Von Mozar

IGNORANCE KILLS...

WATERBUCK

WATERBUCK PUBLISHING LIMITED
LONDON, UK

First published in Great Britain in 2004
by WATERBUCK PUBLISHING

ISBN 0 9548630 0 3

Printed and bound in Great Britain by
BookMarque

Typeset by PABPS London

COVER PHOTO BY KOAX.
POSED BY MODEL.
ALL RIGHTS RESERVED.

WATERBUCK PUBLISHING LIMITED
Waterbuck House, Office 125,
14 Tottenham Court Road
London W1T 1JY

WWW.WATERBUCK.CO.UK

IGNORANCE
KILLS...

This book is dedicated to a good friend:
Anthony Nwigwe R.I.P

Author's acknowledgements

Love and respect to my mum, dad, brothers, sisters, nieces, nephews, uncles, aunties and all my cousins and true friends. Thanks also to everyone in Brixton and everybody else who showed their support, nuff love! (Big up, Smokey.)

Many thanks to Justin, Michael (my big bro), Heidi, Chris, PK, Angie Le Mar, Kemi, Nina, Tracy, Chyna, Theresa, Sadie, Mr Silk and G money for your contributions. Thanks also to you, Jiffy for your criticisms, but wise words.

Thank you to those who refused to help, it only made me stronger!

Last but not least I want to big up myself for believing: "Whatever you can do, or dream you can, begin it. Boldness has genius, power and magic in it. Begin it now!"

One
Von Mozar AKA Nicke Nicks from Bricky.

PRE-ACT

Chapter One

THE WIND BLOWS ICE-COLD up and around the short white skirt worn by Fasard, with her wide hips, large breasts and jet-black hair.

She pulls her skirt further down her bruised, goose-pimpled thighs. It quickly springs back to its previous position.

Fasard places her left hand on her hip and rubs her belly with the right. She is feeling pissed. For over two hours she's been standing on the block, waiting for cars to stop. They pass her in a blur, speeding through the night, taking no notice. You couldn't see them, but in the corners of her eyes are frozen tears.

A car begins to slow down. Fasard pulls the fake leopard-print fur coat over her belly, hoping to hide the evidence of another innocent life that will drop into destruction. She moves quickly over to the street lamp where it's brighter and opens the coat to reveal some more flesh while using her handbag to hide the lump.

The car comes to a dead halt and the door clicks open. Fasard jumps in.

"What's up, babes?" she says casually, with the best sexy smile she can manage.

"It ain't nuttin'," replies the driver as he rubs Fasard's belly.

The rehearsed words from prostitute to squeak seem to freeze in Fasard's throat. She had hoped in the dark of the car the squeak wouldn't realise she was pregnant and maybe she'd get away with just giving oral sex.

Fasard braces herself. She thinks the squeak is going to kick her out of the car, unaware that he had heard a pregnant hooker was giving it up on the block and he had come to get some pregnant-sex.

Still rubbing her stretch-marked, pregnant belly, he says in a whisper, "How much?"

"Erm, erm," Fasard stutters, "Suck and sex, erm twenty, and that includes anal." She pauses and opens her legs as the caressing becomes more vigorous. She wants to tell the squeak to stop, she feels like being sick, but she hasn't turned a squeak all night. She bites on her lip, closes her eyes, then continues while breathing more heavily. "Or ten for just a shine."

The squeak mumbles under his foul-smelling breath while he pulls up Fasard's washed-out T-shirt and sucks on her huge swollen nipples.

"Hol' on, hol' on," begins Fasard with a shocked expression, "you just wanna do it right here?"

"Course, man, course," demands the squeak with his thin lips and small rodent-like eyes. He throws a twenty bill at her, pulls out his penis and drags her head towards it.

Within a few moments, his nuts are busting down

her throat. Fasard swallows and pulls back; she thinks her job is over and gets ready to leave. The squeak throws another twenty bill and grabs her face for a second time.

Chapter Two

THE RAIN IS NOW coming down heavy.

Fasard's jaw begins to hurt as she sucks in vain, trying to make him come for the second time. The squeak pulls out. At last, Fasard thinks, it's over.

"Oi, open your legs," the squeak says coldly.

'Go to hell,' thinks Fasard, but, holding forty bills she's scared he'll take it away.

He penetrates her bareback, with a penis long enough to hit the baby's head. Fasard grabs the seat tightly, her knuckles turning white. She opens her mouth wide and screams out her contraction pains. At first the squeak is unaware; he carries on ruthlessly riding it until a flush of water wets him.

He curses. "Oi, what the rass?" He pulls out his cheesy manhood.

Fasard's head is banging against the car window. Her eyes are bulging, cheeks puffing in and out. She can no longer talk, as screams and low grunts come out instead. Her legs begin to widen and rise at the same time. A wet mass of black hair is protruding between her thighs.

"Oi, wha gwan? Rah shit, the baby!" The squeak panics. "Oi, get your rass-clart self out the car." The squeak stretches over Fasard and clicks open the door.

"No-no, please, help me please," begs Fasard.

A sinister look crosses the squeak's face. "Are you nuts? Get out my car!" He tries pushing her legs over her face, but Fasard holds on for dear life as her screams travel down the empty wet road.

The squeak begins punching and kicking Fasard, cursing incoherently. Fasard can no longer hold on and drops head first into the pouring rain in the late night of December 13th.

Chapter Three

COLD RAIN WETS FASARD'S face; agony makes it twist into a grotesque form. She crawls off the curb backwards until she reaches the bus shelter. Fasard's screams for help penetrate the stillness of the night.

Help is on its way. Fane – slim, tall and bald-headed comes bopping over to her.

"Oi, what the rass did you do?" he accuses.

Fasard's reply is unclear. She is mumbling as she spits phlegm through her nose and mouth.

"Arh, shut up. Get up, man!"

Fasard doesn't move. She points at her belly while trying to catch her breath.

"Oi, did you hear what I said or you're not listening?" Fane gives her one to the head. "Get up. Are you stupid? What's wrong with you?"

Fane drags Fasard up from the ground. "Come on, you stupid bitch. Come on," he yells pulling her away from the bus shelter.

Fasard finally screams out. "Baby, the baby, I'm having the baby!"

The pair stumble to a halt by a lamppost and Fasard holds on for a rest. She grabs her crutch and slides down towards the ground. Fane snatches her up.

"What?! You wanna have the baby on da floor?"

Fasard again slides towards the ground. "Nah, get off me! Just get off me!"

"Arh, you stupid bitch, get up." Fane strong-arms her away from the lamppost towards a grassed area across the road.

Taking small painful steps and still holding her crutch, Fasard tries wriggling out of Fane's grip. "Get off me!" She shouts. "Just, get off me, yeah."

Fane holds Fasard tighter, ignoring her demands and making her slide on her knees a few times before they reach a cockroach-infested house.

Chapter Four

FANE BEATS THE DOOR down. He still has Fasard in an iron grip.

"Come on!" he says to her, as the door, with its crumpling paintwork, opens.

Fane orders a skaghead from the doorway. "Come out the way!" He bundles Fasard towards the floor, which is covered in mess and dirt.

Sweat and rain are pouring off Fasard, but the sweat makes her peel off her clothes. Fasard lies on the floor naked, except for the mini-skirt rolled up under her tits.

In the shadows, bodies circle the room; some piping, others chasing the dragon.

Fane re-enters the room. "What you doing on the floor? I told you to go over to the settee. Oi, Cee-Cee, get up." A skinny cat piping cocaine jumps from the ripped up settee and runs over to a window, holding his crack pipe tightly to his chest.

Fane flicks on the light switch. Brightness floods the space. A couple of cats cover their eyes and run out of the room.

Fasard spits, "Get away from me," as Fane goes to pick her up from the floor. A couple of deep pushing groans fill the room. Suddenly, an innocent life cries.

The newborn had suffered, but the spirit of this child is one of a warrior. It was holding on for dear life. Maybe if it knew what it was coming into, it would have given up.

The baby has natural beauty, a full head of hair, sparkling eyes and fresh baby skin. It's unaware that the ugliness that surrounds it will fight to destroy it. Nothing will protect it, not even its parents.

They had long ago passed that duty of care over to God, government, society or even the people who were masturbating as they watched the baby enter the world.

The baby's parents view life as a one-way train, heading towards death, which they feel they have no power to stop. Mixing that with their everyday suffering produces suicidal and destructive thinking, leading to evil acts of wickedness upon themselves and others. They don't care if the baby suffers and dies, because they're suffering and have to die too. All they want is for the baby to live long enough to get them free housing and a few quid. Of course, they will hide these evil thoughts from others and pretend that they're only doing 'God's work' by going forth and multiplying. They even think that somehow this 'God's work' could bargain them into an effortless existence called Heaven. But don't get it twisted. They feel on a deeper level there is no afterlife, that when you're dead you're dead, forever. No more drugs, alcohol or sex. Your very being disappears spiritually and physically into nothingness. Only bones remain, disgusting memories and a freed conscious-soul.

Chapter Five

MANY MOONS HAS ELAPSED since the harrowing birth of Fasard's child.

After the child was pushed out onto the dirty floor, Fane called an ambulance. At the hospital, they went through an abundance of lies to keep their baby. Not out of love, of course, but to gain profit.

In the past, the boy-dem had taken away two babies, but that was in a different part of the country and under a different name. This time they were determined to keep this one.

She's worth at least one hundred and twenty bills a week in child support, plus a brand new house and everything else the boy-dem take from hard-working people and hand over to individuals infected with laziness and dishonesty.

Their deception worked, but it was the last time Fasard would push out another innocent life for her selfish gain. Something went wrong inside that left her body unable to create life again. On leaving the hospital, she cried from the news and when a nurse asked.

"Oh, what will you call your beautiful baby?" Fasard replied with spiteful anger in her voice, "Brenda... after her grandmother, because she's gonna be a spiteful bitch just like her gran was."

ACT ONE

Chapter Six

THE PASSING OF MANY moons has turned Brenda into a six-year-old. Her eyes sparkle with adventure, still expecting life to deliver something amazing.

The stairs she stands on hopping from foot to foot are grimy, like her everyday surroundings, but that doesn't stop her dreaming maybe this year her prayers to Father Christmas will come true.

Brenda moves down two steps. She stops as they creak; she is scared her mother might catch her and send her back to bed.

With her heart beating fast, she moves as slowly as possible down the last few steps and towards the room that leads to the toilet.

Brenda stops outside the door. Everything sounds quiet, and gradually she turns the door handle and opens the door.

Her eyes sink to the floor on seeing her mother's breasts bouncing up and down.

"Mummy," she says softly. "Mum, mummy," she

repeats a bit harder, without lifting her head from the floor.

Slowly, Fasard looks towards the door, not really believing what she's hearing. Her eyes widen with shock, rapidly turning into hatred.

"What da... What da rass you doing down here?" screams Fasard.

"Get your rass-clart, renking self upstairs!" she adds, as she bobs up and down.

"But mummy I need..." Fasard cuts Brenda off.

"I said..." Fasard doesn't bother finishing her sentence as she jumps off the squeak, reaches for an air freshener can and throws it with force.

The can bounces off the doorframe, missing Brenda by inches. Brenda flees the room.

A surge of anger runs through Fasard's body because she missed her target. She really wants to beat the hell out of her daughter, but she has to hurry up and get this squeak out of the house first.

Fasard flicks her long tangled weave from her face, turns on some music and wiggles back over.

"I'm sorry about that, darling," she says, while meeting the floor with her knees. "The little bitch is just inna."

The squeak doesn't reply as he moves his half-limp penis towards Fasard's mouth. Before she starts to give coitus, she says with as much seduction as she can muster, "Don't worry babes, I'll make it up to you."

Chapter Seven

MANY STREETS AWAY, the early morning coldness blows frosts onto the quiet, abandoned pavements. Opposite a junk-yard are rows of brand new houses. The last house on the corner looks no different from the rest, until you step inside and feel the destructive spirit of the person who lives there. Clothes hang off the banister. The wallpaper is half ripped off the wall. The rank smell of an un-flushed toilet is stifling. The room next to the toilet is about to smell with sex.

"Oi, why don't you go down on me first?"

Fane moves from between the pair of light-skinned legs, holding his penis. "Listen, you know I don't go down."

"Yeah, but when you used to sex my best friend, you went down on her."

Fane is calm; he swallows hard, "I'm gonna be real. I used to go down on your brethren, but I'm not going down on you because your pussy stinks."

The woman squints her eyes. "Yeah, but you wanna hit it doh right?"

"Cause, can't you see I'm wearing a boot? Just shut up and turn around, you little jezz." Fane laughs to himself then sinks his tool. Sweat pours from his back as he sinks it in deeper. The woman crawls forward to escape the full length. Before she escapes, Fane grips her waist and begins pulling her back to him.

His hold slips, the woman escapes, she spins around and clamps her mouth down on his penis.

"Hold on, hold on." Fane pulls out. He peels off the condom. "Al'ight." He puts it back in her mouth and groans. He pulls on her hair.

"Strangle me," she says. "Strangle me."

Fane grabs her long slender neck and starts to squeeze. She sucks even harder. He increases pressure. She grips his butt cheeks. He begins shouting loudly. "You freaking bitch, ah, you bitch."

Chapter Eight

DOWNSTAIRS THE FRONT DOOR opens. Three men enter and climb the stairs.

The first bent-up face belongs to Gize, tall and thin, with cat whiskers for a moustache and thickly plaited hair.

The young lady on her knees sees Gize first as his six-foot-three frame enters the room. She stops sucking, Fane continues strangling. She tries pulling away, but Fane grips her tighter.

"Where you going bitch? Come here."

At that moment, the lick that connects with Fane's temple spins him off his feet and makes him forget his name. The room is silent. The chick sits in the corner with red rings round her neck. Before Gize can open his mouth, Vassal, a short man with a rusty complexion, fully bearded with picky hair appears in the room followed by Dicey, with a shaven head, thick razor bumps on his neck, a bushy scruffy beard and real bad-guy-looks.

Vassal speaks first. "Oi, Gize, the house is empty rudeboy, there's no one else in, rudeboy."

Dicey brushes past Vassal and steps over Fane. "Oi, dis ain't the yout you know, star." Dicey gets no response. "Oi!" He shouts, "Rudeboy, dis ain't the yout rudeboy."

Gize turns to Dicey, "Oi, rudeboy, why you shouting for? I dun told you this yout knows the yout we want. So just cool man, and go chill over there and make me deal wid this."

Dicey pauses before he moves. He looks over at Vassal and mumbles, "Ter, dem boy dere think man's a boy, ya-nah."

Gize turns to the chick on the floor, the mother of his child. "Oi, get up!" Before she moves, she tries to explain the situation. Irritation shadows Gize's face. He bites down on his thin bottom lip, blows through his nose and rushes towards the chick.

"Are you taking man for fool, ah?" Gize has the chick in a neck hold. "Why the rass you didn't answer the phone? You're in here sucking dick and making…" Gize sucks on his teeth, the chick begins struggling, screaming and waving her arms.

"Who you struggling wid, ah, bitch. Ah, who you struggling wid?"

Gize applies more pressure and pins the chick to the wall. Her face turns pale. Vassal jumps in and knocks away Gize's arms as Gize loses control.

"Nah, leave dat blood, leave dat," begs Vassal.

The chick's body slumps to the floor. Gize has a smile on his lips as he spins around to face Vassal and Dicey. He points at Fane. "Why you standing around for? Get him up den, get him up."

Chapter Nine

BRENDA LIES SHAKING IN her bed, eyes full of tears. She jumps with fear at every movement made downstairs as the noise echoes through the thin floorboards. Brenda had seen the craziness in her mother's eyes – the type of madness that leads to a coat-hanger beating. Brenda hates the emotions she is feeling; the emptiness, the fear. What she dislikes the most is that she cannot prevent them from invading her thoughts. She closes her eyes tightly, forcing herself to think about that beautiful dollhouse she saw on TV that she's hoping Father Christmas will bring her. Exciting, happy feelings begin to take over Brenda's thoughts as her mind goes into another world where the worst type of horror is to die and leave behind your earth-generated inner happiness. Brenda's emotions turn sad as she remembers what grown-ups had told her: *we all must die one day, so we can be with Jesus.* Happiness fills her once more. *'Yes, that's the place for me,'* she thinks, *'in heaven where Jesus and God will love me. Jesus loves me, because God told me so,'* says Brenda to herself as warm feelings begin to run through her body.

Brenda then thinks about the stories told at school about God and Jesus. She did not understand most stories, like Jesus dying on the cross and coming back to life. But that was irrelevant, because the part about going to Heaven gave her hope of something better.

Brenda grips her hands together, closes her eyes and begins to pray. "My 'odd, please let me come to Heaven, to be with you and baby Jesus. I promise to be a very good girl, just don't let mummy beat me no more."

A heavy falling sound forces Brenda's eyes to shoot open and she stops praying to prepare herself for a beating. She wraps the covers tightly around her body.

After a while, when the door doesn't burst open, Brenda goes back to praying. "My 'odd, why do mummy not love me like Jesus do? That's why I want to come to Heaven and be with you. Our father in Heaven, give 'r daily bread for I am the glory forever and ever, amen."

Brenda opens her eyes and turns her head towards the window and looks out at the shining stars hanging in the sky. Her happiness returns. Brenda closes her eyes, hoping Father Christmas will still make her wish come true, while hot urine runs down her leg.

Chapter Ten

FANE IS FULLY AWAKE, standing on his feet in the dimly lit bedroom, butt-naked. Cuts and lumps cover his body. He stands with one knee bent, holding his stomach.

"Shit, this yout can take a beating," moans Vassal to no one in particular. Dicey leans off the wall.

"Oi, you know what? Dis is long."

Gize looks at Dicey as if to say: 'Are you stupid?' Then says, "Why is it long? Whhyy, you don't even know he's due to be part of it too."

Fane begins to think, *part of what?* He thought they were cracking his skull because of what he was doing with the babymother.

Fane quickly searches his memory for all the things he has done in the past. It's too many. He locks on to the most recent. *'Oh shit, that was ill.'*

Everyone looks at Fane as he mumbles "I don't know nutting rudeboy. I never do nuffing, star."

"What!" shouts Gize. "What, what did you say?"

Fane holds his head up and repeats, "I said I don't

know nutting, yeah."

Madness enters Gize's eyes as he glances from Vassal to Dicey and asks a rhetorical question: "Who's he talking to?" Then bites down on his lip and leaps towards Fane, his bruised knuckles raised.

The blow cracks Fane's chin. Gize shakes out his fist as Fane hits the floor.

Chapter Eleven

DICEY SUCKS ON HIS teeth and yells, "Why the rass you do that for? Huh? How much times you gonna lick over the yout, without asking him nuffing?"

Gize ignores Dicey and calls his babymother. He has to try and get out of this one fast. He knows that Fane knows nothing. He just wanted help to give Fane a beating for sexing his babymother.

The babymother enters the room with a towel filled with ice pressed on her eye.

"Oi, bitch," begins Gize, "didn't you tell me that this pussy hole knew su'um?"

The babymother removes the ice from her eye and places both hands on her wide hips. She flicks her big-tuff head, then answers, "I didn't tell you that, yeah, I didn't tell you that. I told you to come round and ask him yourself."

"Hold on, you taking man for fool?" Gize's intimidating question isn't convincing to himself or anyone else.

"I bet you that I black the other eye for you... Stop chatting shit."

Dicey jumps into the argument. "I told you this is all long, you get me, rudeboy? You get me?" he says, looking at Gize with his face screwed up. "I swear down, you make man come to your funky babymudars yard on some madness."

"Who you talking to?" says Gize.

Dicey pushes his chest out and steps forward. "What? How you mean who I'm talking to?" Before Gize can reply, Vassal jumps in. "You lot laow dat man, laow dat." Gize looks at Dicey as if to say: 'when you think you're ready, blood, when you think you're ready.'

Dicey flips off Vassal's arm and goes nuts, his arms waving in the air. "Nah, rudeboy, how you mean laow dat, rudeboy? I swear on the Holy Bible I'm gonna get mad, don't get me mad! Look at this dickhead." Dicey points at Gize then continues, "He's knocking out the yout, without asking nuffing. I swear I'm gonna go for my gun. Don't get me mad."

Gize now goes into flipmode, making his arms fly wildly in the air. "Get mad den, get mad. Yeah, get mad, because if it's beef, we'll have beef now den, innit!"

Chapter Twelve

AT THAT, THE BEEF started, because as Gize ended his sentence, he accidentally poked Dicey in the face.

Dicey picks Gize up by the legs and bangs his thin frame against the wall. The babymother runs out of the room.

Vassal shouts, "Oi, you lot, laow that." They ignore him and continue the beef.

Gize elbows Dicey's spine a few times. It's no use, Dicey is too strong. He stiffens his legs then shouts, "Arhhh!" He spins himself and Gize around and crashes towards the chest of drawers.

Dicey holds Gize in a bear hug and unleashes a head butt. Gize's nose cracks, but the pain gives him some extra strength. He somehow gets out of the bear hug and starts throwing blow after blow. The first few connect, but are no good. Dicey shakes them off and lands a few left-right upper cuts. The punches daze Gize, but he's much stronger than he looks. He begins to skip around, dodging the soft blows Dicey is throwing. Dicey sees it coming, but it's too quick. CLAP! Straight on the jaw. Dicey spins towards the door with fear in his eyes: he knows he's beaten. He feels he would have won if he got through with a knockout blow, but now it's too late.

Gize jumps in for the kill. Just before he does, Fane springs to his feet holding his trousers. He runs for the half-open window, taking everyone by surprise by diving out headfirst.

The window shatters with the impact of his legs. The breaking of the glass reminds the thugs of the real reason they are there.

They jump to the window, expecting to see Fane curled up on the ground. All they can say is, "Ter," as they watch him quickly limp away from the third floor window and down the road, making his escape.

Chapter Thirteen

A CHILLY BREEZE BLOWS through the twenty-storey block filled with cramped homes. A few lights are on amongst the two hundred or so windows. Bang in the middle of the block, the dimmest light of all shines through a thick, grimy, orange curtain; behind it, Fasard is still entertaining.

"How dat feel, ha? How dat feel?" Fasard bites down on her lip, grips the torn up black settee and moans. "Oh give it to me harder, oh, harder."

The squeak moves in and out faster and faster. Sweat is pouring from both bodies as deep bassline music pumps and vibrates.

Out in the hallway, Fane slams the front door and staggers to the sitting room entrance. He braces himself against the wall trying to catch his breath. Blood runs down from his eyes over his bruised face and swollen lips.

Holding his rib cage, he nudges the sitting room door open. A static awkwardness occurs that seems to silence the loud, bassy music and draw the walls in, reducing the room to the size of a prison cell.

"Fane, Fa...ane!" screams Fasard. The squeak pulls out quicker than Brenda ran out of the room earlier.

"Oh shit, Fane, oh shit," screams Fasard as she runs over to her man. Fane falls into her arms. She leads him over to a soiled sofa.

The squeak has finished fumbling with his clothes; his T-shirt is on backwards and his jeans are dropping off his waist. He picks up his coat and makes for the door.

"Oi, where you think you going?" The man freezes.

"So what, aren't you gonna pay what you owe?" demands Fasard, looking over her shoulder.

The man reaches into his pocket and pulls out a fist-ful of bills. He clenches his fist for a moment, turns to face Fasard and says. "Ter, sick," then throws down two bills onto the see-through coffee table and leaves.

Chapter Fourteen

FASARD'S ATTENTION MOVES away from Fane. She grabs the money and mumbles to herself. In that very moment, it seems as though Fasard has totally forgotten Fane's presence.

She walks out of the room and brings back an old sock filled with ice. She presses it against Fane's eye and he screws up his face from the pain, then speaks. "Dey tried to kill me, babes. Yeah, dey tried to murk me."

"But why doh?" Asks Fasard.

Fane closes his eyes. A few teardrops fall as the memory of his uncle's words come back to him. At the time, he interpreted those words as opinions, now he realises they identify reality. His uncle had said, 'The purpose of life is happiness and only true happiness comes from creative actions that benefit yourself and others.' Those words had given him dreams of becoming a research scientist, but the streets wouldn't allow it. They took him into the world of robbing, shotting, drug-taking and loose women. For a while, Fane thought, the streets were proving his uncle's statement wrong. The happiness he got from his destructive actions began to give him everything: fancy cars, pretty chains and fat-arse girls. And they came with very little effort. But now he hates the streets for what they took from him. He swallows some spit and speaks in a low voice. "I took what weren't mines."

Fasard doesn't bother to ask what he took. She slides behind him, still holding the ice to his eye and caresses his head.

Chapter Fifteen

THE STARS OUTSIDE SHINE bright, and light up parts of the road where street lamps no longer shine.

The three thugs are on the street corner. The beef is over, but Gize is trying his best to convince Dicey.

"Listen, rudeboy, why you think he ran off for? If he never knew nuffing he wouldn't run off. Trust me rudeboy, my babymother knows where he lives, rudeboy, trust me."

Dicey knows Gize is scheming, but he wants to release his anger onto something or someone due to losing the beef, and soon enough he feels he'll get the people he's after and get revenge on Gize.

"Where's dat, bitch?" asks Dicey, "'cause I swear down, she better know where he lives."

Gize smiles. "Just cool, man. She does man, she does."

From the blackness of the alleyway she emerges, hips hidden underneath an ankle-length winter coat.

"Dere she is," says Vassal. Dicey opens the car doors and the thugs bundle in, waiting for her to reach them.

The babymother stops outside the car clutching her coat, as if waiting for a gentleman to open the door. The electric window winds down.

"What!? Get in the car den." Gize's order is full of fake, frustrated anger.

Slowly she reaches out, unlocks the latch and jumps in. For a moment, the car is quiet until Dicey blows out air with anxiety and asks, "Ter, which part of the town does this prick live?"

Gize turns to his babymother and repeats the question.

"I told you already," replies babymother, half cocking her eye and giving a sad little girl expression. Gize raises his voice.

"Oi, don't mess wid me ya-nah. I wanna know if it's the bottom, middle or top part of the lane."

Looking straight ahead with a pissed-off sulky look, she answers. "Well sort of in the middle, innit? The road opposite the petrol station."

Gize looks at her with disgust in his eyes. He wants to give her a backhander. He holds it down, shakes his head from side to side then lets out a "Ter."

Dicey moves the car into first gear and disappears into the night.

Chapter Sixteen

THE NIGHT OUTSIDE FANE'S window seems calm. His view stretches for a few miles west, showing the lights of the city in their full beauty. Every now and then, a lone car shoots down the main road without stopping. This puts Fane at ease. He's sure the baby-mother will bring the thugs to his yard. When he told Fasard this, she stopped caressing his head and went into panic mode.

She re-enters the room with a can of beer and asks, with fear in her voice, "So where we gonna go?"

Fane replies calmly. "I don' know, let me think."

But the pain he can feel running up and down his face, interrupts his thinking and to make it worse, Fasard carries on asking the same question.

"FANE!" she screams. "Where the hell are we gonna go?" She staggers to her feet and takes a gulp of the poison, pulling at Fane's string vest.

"Oi, are you listening to me?"

The pain from his injuries seems to disappear as he vents his frustration on Fasard's face. One bitch lick crumples her to the floor.

"You, bastard," she shouts. She spins on her bottom, legs in the air, trying to give Fane a kung-fu kick.

He holds her right leg and flips her away. "Move, you idiot. Are you stupid?" Fane pauses, feeling remorse towards Fasard. He looks down at her. "Get up."

Fasard hollers, "Leave me alone, you bastard!" Fane screws up his face. He only wants to hold her and be held and for just one moment to cry away the sadness that bleeds within his heart.

He repeats himself, but this time with bitterness. "Get up, get up!"

Resting on the sofa with her legs wide apart, Fasard challenges, "Why don't you make me, you piece of shit?"

Fane's eyes widen as he spits, "You want me to make you, yeah. You want me to make you." This isn't a question. He reaches down and pulls her up by the blouse, holds her close to him as if to kiss her. "You want somewhere to go." This is not a question either. Fane continues. "Because it ain't nuffing stopping me throwing you out this pussyclart window." Fane nudges Fasard's body towards the window then shakes her back and forth. "Then you will go to hell. Then I will go to prison. Don't get me mad."

Fasard looks in his eyes and she wants to scream, *'do it then, do it, kill me,'* but the madness that stares back suggests he might just do it.

Chapter Seventeen

"DON'T DO IT, BRUV," warns Vassal as Dicey contemplates jumping the red light to shake off the boydem behind him. Dicey slows down and stops at the traffic lights. He taps on the steering wheel and waits. Vassal looks back at Dicey and offers more advice.

"Yeah, it's better dat, blud, trust me you don't wanna look bait, it's long."

Dicey doesn't reply but looks straight ahead as his thoughts drift to the gun inside the air bag compartment. He told himself long ago if the feds ever stopped him while he was driving with his stick he wouldn't ramp to pepper their skin. But that was when Dicey didn't respect his life or other lives. Since he started shotting and stacking a little fortune, his outlook is now changing. Dicey wants to get out of the grime, start spending and enjoy life.

"Oi, bro," begins Gize, from the back seat, "if you make the feds stops us ya-nah, you better empty your clip on them ya-nah, you get me? No long ting, 'cause I'm not riding no ten years."

Dicey comes back to reality. The destructive force of his world is upon him. He knows he can't back down. He stays cool and doesn't respond to Gize's warning.

He looks calmly into the rear view mirror, puts the car into first gear and waits for the green light.

Chapter Eighteen

HE MOVES OFF, STEERING the car into the far lane. The first set of traffic lights behind Dicey's car turn green also, letting the police car through. The boy-dem steadily drive down on Dicey, who drives around the bend that connects to the main road near where Fane lives. Cutting through the red light on the corner of the bend, the feds follow up behind them.

"Shit!" swears Vassal. "What's wrong with these boy-dem, man?" He questions with fear in his voice. Gize takes note.

"Just cool, man. Hold this stick." Gize pulls two guns from under the seat and passes one to Vassal. Vassal's hand shakes a little.

"Why you giving me this for? We ain't gonna need this, da boy-dem ain't stopping us." Vassal tries to control the panic in his voice.

The babymother speaks, "Um, I think they're about to stop us you know."

Gize speaks to Dicey. "Oi, Dice, don't stop da car, wors' ways me and Vas will buss the shots."

Dicey looks in the rear view mirror and meets Gize's stony, determined gaze and knows he has to represent, but he also has to protect his old school brethren, Vassal. "Just cool, man. If they stopping us we're all bussing. Oi, Vas, give me the strap." Vassal's blood pressure comes down as he almost throws the gun into Dicey's lap.

"Listen, yeah, Vas. If we get stopped I'll give it back." Dicey throws the gun under his seat. "Anyway, da boy-dem due to not even stop us." As Dicey ends his sentence, the blue lights whirl around without the siren sounding.

Chapter Nineteen

"ALRIGHT, FANE, WAIT, WAIT." Fasard scrambles from the floor and out of Fane's grip. "I've got an idea, yeah."

Fasard pauses, and Fane shouts, "Talk!"

"Maybe we can go to my sister's yard." Fane stares silently at Fasard and uses what brain cells he has left to recall the sister.

'Oh, that freak.'

Fasard's sister, Caprishus, a.k.a. Auntie Caprishus, was once married with eight children, until she left her husband for a woman. She is now back with her 'no-good' husband after eight years of lesbian love.

"Nah bun dat, bun dat," retorts Fane.

Fasard feels hurt and lashes out. Her nails leave streaks of blood on Fane's chest. His shirt flaps open as he goes after her.

She almost makes it out the door, screaming. "No Fane, no, no, Fane, please."

Too late. With a flying kick, Fane catches her in the

ribs. She spins past the door and hits her head on the table.

Survival instincts kick in as she seizes an opportunity and lands her foot between Fane's legs. As he crumbles to the floor, she runs out of the room and into the kitchen. A moment later, Fane steps in after her. Fasard doesn't realise as she searches for a knife.

"What the rass you think you doing?"

Fasard spins around, holding the sink for support, "Just leave me alone, yeah. Leave me alone or..."

Bopping his head up and down Fane walks towards her and says, "Or what, ah, or what?!"

Fasard points at him. "Just leave me alone."

Fane doesn't see it coming. He replies, "Yeah, you think you bad, yeah, you think you rass-clart bad, um gonna bruck up..." His words end there. Fasard grabs the long bread knife out of the sink and sinks it into him twice. Fane falls to his knees holding his chest and curls into a ball. Fasard flees the room without looking back.

Chapter Twenty

OUTSIDE, THE TWO COPS move cautiously towards the parked car. The registration check came back with a report that the car was possibly involved in an armed bank robbery, but for some reason the report has not yet been confirmed. So the two officers take it upon themselves to do the stop without waiting for confirmation that the stop should be carried out by the armed SO19 response team.

The one wearing the black waterproof coat stops and talks into his radio clipped to his coat collar. The one with the balding head advances, stopping outside the blacked-out window and tapping softly, then a bit harder. The window slowly winds down.

"What's da problem?" Demands Dicey without looking at the officer.

The officer speaks one of his rehearsed police monologues.

"And how can you tell that, by the way I was driving?"

The officer avoids the question and demands to know where Dicey, and a car smelling of marijuana is going at this time of the night.

Dicey answers with more attitude, "Home, innit?"

The officer fires back with, "Where's home?"

"Ter, up the road, man," replies Dicey.

The officer has had enough. He orders Dicey who is now a suspect out of the car in the usual police manner, calm but firm.

"Who you talking to?! You think man's a boy?!" Dicey sucks on his teeth, "Man ain't coming out no car, are you stupid?"

The officer remains calm and demands to search the car for illegal substances. He asks Dicey if he has anything on him he shouldn't have.

"Yeah, man's got weed, what?" answers Dicey.

The officer isn't ready for this. His training in Police College didn't teach him how to handle a poverty-driven mentality. He's baffled; he pauses in thought, not seeing his partner trying to signal him away from the car, until it is too late.

Chapter Twenty-One

SIRENS FOLLOWED BY HARSH braking and skidding are heard as vans zoom around the rookie police officer. Doors fly open and the boy-dem jump out shouting, "DON'T MOVE, ARMED POLICE!" They have their Heckler & Cock MP5s pointed at the car.

Time slows down for Dicey as he contemplates what move to make.

He puts the car into gear and shoots forward into a parked police van. The impact throws everyone towards the windscreen. Dicey's chest hits the steering wheel and his gun falls into his lap.

The screams from the boy-dem continue. Dicey knows it's time to become fully real to this destructive nature, which conscious man was never meant to be a part of.

Dicey unclicks his door and sets it off. He gets to squeeze off two shots. He will never know if they peppered any of the boy-dem as the return fire brings him off his feet and towards the cold concrete.

Unnecessary gunfire continues for a few more seconds. When it finally stops, the outside of the car is surrounded with smoke. Nothing moves.

The policeman in charge shouts, "HOLD YOUR FIRE." They advance steadily, some circling around to the other door. The three-finger count is given, then both doors are swung open with guns aimed at the bodies.

Sixteen bullets hit the car. Inside there is no splattered blood, but the babymother and Vassal are stone dead. Her from a single shot to the head and him from four shots to the body. The one that hit him on the collarbone travelled all the way down to his heart.

Gize is sitting on the left side of the babymother. He still has his gun held tight in his hand, eyes staring into space. He could move but doesn't, not until the boy-dem disarm him and throw him in the van. In jail, he would tell stories about how he peppered two of the boy-dem before they brought him down with two shots to the legs.

During the next hour, more higher-ranking officers appeared as the lower ranking ones came and went. Eventually , all that was left was blue and white police tape squaring off the main road around the incident, with two officers standing guard on either side.

Chapter Twenty-Two

BRENDA'S BEDROOM DOOR flies open, the hairs on the back of her neck stand on end, as a half-dressed Fasard begins to yell. "Bitch, get your nasty self up. Now!" Fasard spins back around and leaves the room in haste.

Brenda doesn't move. Fasard runs back into the room, eyes now wider than wide.

"Oi, bitch, you never hear what I just said?" Fasard drags the sheets off Brenda.

"You nasty little, stinking renking bitch. Piss up the whole of the bloodclart bed." Fasard reaches for a coat hanger and grips Brenda by the collar and pulls her out of the bed.

"Mummy, please, no." Brenda begins to cry. "Please, mummy, please." Brenda wriggles out of her grip and tries to escape. A lash connects with her bottom. "Ah, mummy." Another lash makes her spin around and run back towards her bed, grabbing the sheets to shield herself.

Fasard pulls away the thick blanket, leaving Brenda

holding a thin undersheet. She begins whipping her daughter ruthlessly, chasing her all around the room.

Chapter Twenty-Three

FANE LIES SPREAD-EAGLED on the kitchen floor. He can move but doesn't want to. He opens his eyes, hearing the banging from upstairs.

He now remembers how and why he's bleeding. Looking at the grease-covered ceiling, anger rises inside him. Fane knows that if he wants he can easily kill Fasard, but thinks, why waste his strength, what would be the use? She'll be dead in about twenty years time and dead is dead; it's all the same whether it's now or a hundred years from now. He knows the immutable laws of reality will bring Fasard to a horrible end, like they do with everything else that isn't fully honest. A madman's smile grows across his face as a strange feeling of peace comes over him. *'All those past destructive actions, done in vain.'* Hearing Fasard dragging Brenda down the stairs interrupts his thoughts. One last urge to stop Fasard come and go.

Fane grins as he watches Fasard throw Brenda into the wooden banister, spin her around and push her towards the open door.

Fasard uses so much force slamming the door it doesn't shut properly.

Fane watches the door slowly creaking open. He lies perfectly motionless as if waiting for death. He can't take the struggle of life any more; there is too much pressure, too much dishonesty. The thought of those thugs splitting his wig put another madman's smile on his face.

Fane is ready to die and make his final escape.

Chapter Twenty-Four

IT IS STILL DARK outside when Fasard reaches the brick house. She bangs hard on the door to get the occupants' attention over the loud music. The door opens. Before Fasard sees the person, the strong scent of weed hits her.

"Oh, hi, darling," Fasard springs out her arms and steps forward for a hug. "Is mummy in?"

"Yeah," says Shun, with his curly hair, smooth skin and hazel eyes.

He steps back and opens the door fully. Fasard turns around and Brenda comes into view.

"Come on." Fasard grips Brenda's head and throws her towards the doorway, following up behind. She shuts the door and turns to Shun again. "Mum's upstairs, yeah?" Shun simply nods his head.

Brenda, now abandoned, stays silent. Her thoughts are on Father Christmas bringing the dollhouse. She's sure that this year he will bring it. The feeling of being unable to get back home makes her start to cry.

A voice from the top of the stairs calls out to Shun.

"Oi, what you doing to her?"

"Um, nuffing man, she just started to cry."

"Why, what's wrong with her?"

"I don't know. She's just crying."

Shun's big sister, Salma approaches, Brenda. "Come on, don't cry, come, come up stairs."

Brenda stops her tears and follows, hand-in-hand, up the steps.

Chapter Twenty-Five

TIME IS PUSHING INTO the early morning. The four-storey house where Brenda is beginning to relax is wide awake as if it's early afternoon.

The children surrounding Brenda have nothing productive to stimulate their minds. Therefore, their psychology operates without any respect, discipline or honesty.

Brenda stares around the room at her cousins as they smoke weed, drink alcohol and use swear words. This fills her with excitement.

There are four cousins present, and another person who isn't Brenda's relation; he's making the most noise, declaring how he knocked out a squeak late last night with one punch.

Brenda's second oldest cousin shouts over his shoulder from in front of the TV. "Oi, Tyrell, shut your mouth man. You can't even knock out your dinner, you wally."

The room falls into silence, then laughter. Tyrell feels shamed and hurt, responding. "What, who you talking to, you cat?"

"'Old on, cuzzy." Nits rises from the TV. "Are you stupid? Mine how you're talking you know? I will slap you to death. You're a licckle man."

Tyrell gives off a nervous laugh. He forgot who he was talking to.

"Ah, just cool man, just cool cuz, man."

"How you mean just cool? Respect su'um, man." Nits kicks past Tyrell's knees, grabs up his coat and walks out of the room.

Brenda watches the door close and waits for a while, hoping her cousin will come back in so she can see some more excitement. He doesn't, so she gets off the leather footstool, turns to Shun and says, "I wanna go toilet."

Shun doesn't take his eyes off the computer game as he replies, "It's downstairs, man, go downstairs."

Chapter Twenty-Six

BRENDA HADN'T BEEN in a house with so many doors and stairs before. The house felt like a maze.

To find her way back, she opened at least four doors until she found the right one.

The atmosphere in the room has changed with the loud music off and the TV on. No one is talking and the lights are off.

Brenda steps forward. Tyrell notices her.

"Should she be in here?"

"Just cool, rudeboy, she's big enough now," says Azher, Brenda's third oldest cousin.

"Yeah, how old is she?"

"What, she's about ten, innit?" Azher looks at Brenda for confirmation, but she stays quiet.

"Anyway, listen, man– I started having sex at eight, you get me? So just cool, man."

Brenda sits on the leather stool, experiencing feelings she has never felt before as a sex orgy takes place on TV. She keeps watching the door, expecting her mother to burst in and spoil this new experience, but

Fasard is at the top of the house getting drunk on rum and coke.

Brenda's thoughts about her mother have now disappeared as the sounds from the TV fill the room like surround sound. The added sound is actually Tyrell and Salma, who has juicy thick thighs, meaty childbearing hips, a tiny waist and a small bust. Her complexion is smooth and she has a prominent, pretty nose.

Salma's legs are in the air with Tyrell in between. She's screaming over the TV volume. Azher is watching closely and playing with himself. Shun just sits there playing his computer game, like he's seen it all before.

The room fills up with the smell of sex – smelly sex; unwashed cheesy pussy and dick sex.

A few more screams and it's over. Tyrell pulls up his jeans and rolls off Salma. She rolls down her skirt and slips on her knickers.

"Oi, your little cousin was watching hard, boy, like she wanted to join in," says Tyrell.

"Don't be silly, man, she's too young for you," replies Salma.

"Yeah, I bet she ain't too young for your little brother doh." Tyrell looks in Shun's direction.

"But they're cousins, man. What's wrong with you?"

"So, you're going like you ain't sexed one of your cousins before?" Salma falls silent. She looks at Azher. He shrugs his shoulders.

"Hey, Brenda, come here. Do you wanna do what

we were doing on the floor with Shun?"

Brenda makes no reply. Salma pulls down Brenda's pink and white leggings. Brenda stands stiffly with only her frilly white knickers on.

"Oi, Shun, come here den." Shun puts down the computer game and moves over towards Brenda, now lying on the sofa bed.

He climbs between Brenda's legs, which Salma and Tyrell are holding open.

Chapter Twenty-Seven

BRENDA WAKENS IN a different room on a king-size bed. Shun's leg is sprawled over her body. The sheets are kicked onto the floor except for a tea-stained spreadsheet wrapped around Shun's other leg and tangled in-between the two bodies at the foot of the bed.

Brenda flings off Shun's leg and sits up. She looks down at her two younger cousins. She can't remember their names; there are so many brothers and sisters. Eight in total. Sometimes the mother would forget their names too. She would end up calling out all the names of her six boys until she got to the right name of the boy she wanted.

The bedroom door opens and a crying toddler walks in. Her baby grower is dirty down the front and open at the crutch, revealing no nappy. She stands there staring at Brenda through her tear-filled eyes, holding an action figure with its head missing.

Shun wakes and kicks one of his little brothers to feed their baby sister.

"Oi, Gitty, make her bottle, man."

"Nah, man. Ask Chase, man."

"Get up, you, fool." Shun kicks Gitty a bit harder.

"You see, man." Gitty wakes up and rolls out of the bed. He looks down at Chase, planning to make his younger brother, by one year, pay for this. "Oh, why can't he do it, man?" No one answers Gitty. "You see you lot are flipping idiots, you know." Gitty slugs over to his baby sister, grabs her hand and leaves the room.

Brenda lies back down and stares up at the foreign ceiling, Shun's voice comes to her. "Oi, Brenda, Happy Christmas."

A smile breaks across her face. She almost forgot it was Christmas. Her smile disappears as she starts to feel things she can't express. Brenda hates the fact that she has to lie at school about getting Christmas presents. She hates that nothing good ever happens to her. But most of all she hates feeling this way. Just for once, can't something good happen? Brenda's heart sinks, but she still holds onto the hope that somehow Father Christmas knows where she is, and will bring her that beautiful dollhouse.

In the back of her mind, she knows this year she will have to lie again. Brenda closes her eyes and dreams of a life without lying. A loud snapping bang interrupts her. Brenda wakes up.

Chapter Twenty-Eight

BEFORE ANYONE HAS TIME to leave their rooms and see what the noise is about the police have Nits handcuffed and are dragging him up the stairs.

"Which one is your room?!" demands officer Palooka, tall, dark but not very handsome.

"Don't watch dat, man, the cuffs are too tight, man."

Officer Palooka takes no notice of Nits' plea. "Listen, sonny," he begins, with a frown on his face, "you either tell me which room is yours, or we'll tear this whole house apart."

"What?! Go do it," replies Nits, emphasising that this threat means nothing to him. The house is mash-up anyway.

Officer Palooka looks pissed. He doesn't want to turn the house upside down. That just means more paperwork; but that's part of the job, so he gives the order.

He's about to send Nits back to the van with officer Biggs when a huge-chested woman appears at the top of the stairs in a pink dressing gown done halfway up.

It's Nits' mum, Caprishus. She speaks, revealing no front teeth. "He don't live here, yeah. What you doing in here? Get out my house."

"Now, miss, please…" Caprishus cuts Palooka off.

"Don't bother 'miss please' me, yeah, just get out my house yeah. Come bruck down my door, yeah, for what and for what?"

Palooka's face fills with anger. "Well if you shut up for one minute." He stops himself from adding, *'you stupid bitch.'* "You will see we have a warrant to search this premises."

Actually, because of their rush to find evidence, Palooka doesn't have a warrant. All he has is a copy of a requested warrant.

"Where's the warrant? Show me the warrant?"

He flicks out a piece of paper from his back pocket with confidence, knowing that it's very rare for a poverty-minded person to inspect an official-looking document in all its small print.

Caprishus glances over it and continues, "He don't live here anyway. He don't live here."

Palooka breathes easy. He has gotten away with it again.

"That's not what he told us. He is connected to a very serious crime."

Nits begins to struggle.

"Mum, they're lying, mum, they're lying, I swear down. Let me go, man."

"Get him out of here," orders Palooka.

Four officers grab Nits off his feet and swing him outside. Caprishus begins to say something else, but

Palooka ignores it and pushes past her. He looks down at Shun and Brenda. He smirks, then pushes past them too.

Chapter Twenty-Nine

BRENDA WATCHES PALOOKA and his helpers ransack her aunt's home. She wonders what her auntie can do to stop it. The boy-dem showed a piece of paper from a judge giving them authority to use force against individual property rights. That is all that matters and that's all they need to mash up people's yard.

Brenda's mind drifts back to her hope that Father Christmas will still bring the dollhouse, but it is fading fast. Brenda's heart sinks deeper into her stomach. She wonders if Father Christmas really exists or if he only exists for those that have a family that love them.

Another outburst from her Auntie Caprishus upsets Brenda's thoughts, but she smiles– at least she's getting some entertainment.

After two hours, the boy-dem stop their ransacking, leaving empty-handed. Caprishus had cussed them until she lost her voice, and that was the end of Brenda's dose of stimulation.

The next sixteen months flashed by with much more stimulation, and when Brenda had to leave the house, she kicked and cried. Fasard punched and slapped her until she let go of the staircase.

Brenda then blocked out from her memory almost everything and everyone at the house. To remember made her sad. Only two memories stayed in her sub-conscious: Shun and that beautiful dollhouse, which she never received.

ACT TWO

Chapter Thirty

BY THE TIME BRENDA reaches the age of twelve, her womanly figure has blossomed, kept nourished by the food she has to steal from supermarkets. Her hips are wide and her waist is small and trim, with her chest grown to perfection. Brenda's jet-black curly hair seems almost synthetic in contrast with her naturally beautiful, flawless complexion.

The month is April and Brenda is on spring break from school. At 12 p.m. she jumps out of bed and walks downstairs towards the kitchen. Brenda stops. The door on her right has just enough light peeping through the thick red curtain to illuminate Fasard, still in a drunken sleep, tossing and turning on the dirty sofa, which is filled with holes.

Brenda sucks on her teeth and walks into the kitchen, pours salt and water into a cup, then returns to the bathroom.

The bathroom wallpaper is peeling off the wall. There is no toilet seat or flooring because the tiles have slipped away one by one a long time ago. Brenda looks into the half-broken mirror perched on top of the sink.

She dips her toothbrush into the cup and begins brushing her teeth. Brenda's dream of getting that dollhouse has disappeared. She dreams now of a real house, a big mansion somewhere. She wants to be rich – super rich – that is her idea for the happiness she craves. Brenda takes a swig of the salt-water, gargles and spits. She washes her face then goes back downstairs to look for lotion.

Her eyes are darting around the room where Fasard lies asleep. An object comes into view on the coffee table in front of the sofa. She moves closer. It's just an ashtray, filled with cigarette butts. Unable to think where to look next, Brenda begins to shake her mother. "Mum, mummy, mum." Fasard rolls over and makes a "Mmmm," sound.

Brenda carries on shaking. "Mummy, mummy." Fasard is jolted out of her sleep. "What, what, what is it?!" Her eyes are red like cherries.

"I want some lotion."

Fasard wants to lash out, but controls herself.

"If you want lotion go buy lotion." Fasard rubs the sleep out of her face.

"But, mum, you got lotion. Can't I have some of your lotion, please?"

Fasard looks up at her daughter, "I said no, get out and leave me alone, before me and you have su'um in here."

Brenda mumbles underneath her breath, "Bitch! I hate you," and leaves the room.

Chapter Thirty-One

BRENDA FLICKS OFF her long, bedtime T-shirt and squeezes into a pair of jeans. She throws on a waist-high jean jacket and worn out footwear. Brenda searches all the rooms again for lotion. Nothing. She's feeling stressed and wants a fag, so she goes back downstairs to get some dog ends out of the ashtray.

Fasard is fast asleep, but now has an orange and white, picture-pattern blanket wrapped around her. Brenda watches Fasard roll over onto her side. She steps through the door and heads for the ashtray, stopping for a moment to look at her mother. A silver cigarette packet sticks awkwardly out from the cushion.

Adrenaline rushes through Brenda's body. She moves towards the fags without taking her eyes off her mother. She fumbles with the packet until she gets one out – its badly squashed, but it doesn't matter. She puts it in the top pocket of her jeans jacket and freezes as Fasard rolls onto her back. But she doesn't wake.

Brenda relaxes. She's about to make her way out of the room when a gold buckle hidden underneath a small pile of clothes on a wooden chair catches her eye. It's Fasard's handbag where she keeps her lotion. Brenda unclips it with eyes fixed on her mother. She fumbles in the bag. No lotion. But she finds something else – a purse stuffed with money. She can't believe it because her mother always hides paper money down her underwear. Brenda's hand shakes as she removes forty bills from the bundle and, without looking back down at her mother, she throws the bag back underneath the clothes and flees the house. She steps out onto the grey stone landing of her housing estate. She begins walking without really knowing where to go first. She has never held so much money so she feels rich for the moment.

Her first stop is a burger, chicken and ribs place. The last time she ate fast food was when one of her mother's 'boyfriends' gave her his leftovers.

Chapter Thirty-Two

BRENDA SWALLOWS THE FOOD as if someone is about to take it away from her. She looks up from her tray at a group of young males who are making noise. They're all wearing the usual street gear for 'Poverty-Driven Children,' hoodies, low caps and footwear costing from fifty to a hundred and ten bills.

Brenda recognises the one leading the crew, but isn't sure he would remember her. One member of the crew walks over to where she is sitting with a bop in his step and trousers sagging low off his waist. He speaks before he sits. Brenda looks up, chewing on her food.

"Sorry, say that again," mumbles Brenda.

"You listenin'? I said you look good and I know you like what you see. So give me your number and we link up, you get me?"

Brenda thinks, *number what number? Does he mean my house door number? That's the only number I can give him.*

"So what you saying, you gonna give me your mobile?"

Brenda shakes her head and says, "No, I haven't got

one."

The other replies, "So what about a land line?"

"I ain't got one of them either."

"All right, all right you take my number, yeah, cause trust me I'm not even gonna lie. You're the, boom-ting. I would make you my wifey straight." Brenda begins to blush as the guy starts to hold and rub her hand. Her eyes dart over to the counter where Shun is standing and looking at her. He recognises his cousin, so calmly he bops over. "Oi, my, yout, what you doing?" Demands Shun.

The youth turns around, puzzled. "What?! I'm talking to this young ting, innit."

"Oi, nah, bruv. Step, bruv, step."

This youth knows the reputation of Shun. He isn't scared but he can't understand why Shun wants to break his legs. "How you mean?!! I'm talking to this chick, innit?"

"Oi, Bruv. I said step, blud."

The youth doesn't move. "Oi, rudeboy, just cool, man."

Shun's face turns hostile. "Oi, bruv. Are you stupid? I'll blaze you ya-nah, bruv. Oi, you're lucky I ain't got my stick on me, I would lick you down out here."

A crying sound seems to fill the youth's voice, "Why, why? Just because I'm talking to this chick?"

"Yesss, I will lick you down for less than nutting, rudeboy."

The youth gets mad and flips his arms towards Shun's face. "Ah, move, man, you taking man for some boy."

Shun doesn't blink as he easily picks up the youth from the seat and bangs him into the wall. The rest of the crew get involved and break it up.

The youth begins to point and shout. "Watch-watch-watch!" His pride is dented as he walks off with his arms swinging and stepping like he has a stone in his left shoe. Shun looks back over at Brenda and gives his straight-toothed smile and says in a smooth tone, "So wha, give me a hug den, cuzzy."

Brenda shoots up from her seat and grabs him under his armpits. They hold the embrace for a few moments then release each other. Shun keeps hold of her shoulder with his right arm.

"Hey, I ain't seen you for long you know, cuz."

Brenda smiles her nervous smile but doesn't take her gaze from Shun's eyes as he goes on. "You've grown into a big girl now doh, innit?" Still no reply. Brenda just blushes and nods her head.

"Anyway, what you finished there now, yeah?"

Brenda nods and picks up her milkshake. Shun puts his arm around her neck and leads her out of the restaurant. He leaves his crew behind as if he wasn't even with them.

Chapter Thirty-Three

BRENDA'S HEART IS BEATING fast as she steps through the doors underneath Shun's arm. The whirlwind of his bad boy aura and his good looks have her hooked. Like most girls, she's in love with the hazel eyes set deep within the cool skin of Shun's sweet boy face. Shun looks at Brenda out of the corner of his eye. He can't help noticing her beauty and the maturity of her body.

For the first time, Brenda communicates with words. "Um... Shun, you know where I can get some weed?"

The couple stop outside the restaurant window. Shun looks at Brenda with a serious face. "What, you're burning it down den, yeah?"

"Yeaaah," replies Brenda in a low, unconcerned way, smiling from ear to ear as if declaring she's part of some special race of individuals.

Shun smiles then shocks Brenda by saying, "Oi, don't think smoking weed is good ya-nah, it mashes you up in the end. 'Old on, I saw a show that done some research on that shit and it's all true." Shun points to his chest, "Ter, but man like me, yeah, I'm real. I don't give a fuck about my health or life, if I dead, I just dead." Shun shakes his head, "It's nuffing."

Shun's last statement puts fear in Brenda's heart. It always does when death is mentioned. This is weird, because on one level death seems to her like the only escape from her shitty surroundings. But on another level, if there is no life after death, she'd be dead forever and would have missed out on the happiness she feels one day will be hers.

Brenda's thoughts are interrupted as Shun leads her across the road towards the drug-base, and those exciting feelings she used to feel as a child begin to flood her again. She holds onto Shun's arm tightly and follows.

Chapter Thirty-Four

SHUN'S ROOM IS HALF-EMPTY, just a single bed in the corner with clothes piled in the opposite one. At the foot of the bed, a small TV is stacked on top of a hi-fi system with trainers and a game-station surrounding it. The TV and music are blaring. Brenda sits on the bed with her back to the wall and legs swinging off the edge.

Shun enters the room with two bottles of alcohol and a wooden chair, which he pulls up to the window ledge and lays the weed, rizlas, cigarettes and the bottles of poison on it.

He looks over his shoulder at Brenda. "What, you want me to bill up for you, yeah?" Brenda nods. Shun begins to roll and lick and says with excitement in his eyes, "Dis will buzz you up, ber high grade ya-nah. Yeah, this weed will lick off your head, star."

Brenda begins to smile as the anticipation fills her; the tension and bad feelings are about to disappear for a while.

By now, Shun has rolled two joints. He lights the

first one and hits it hard and long, blowing smoke from his nostrils then out of his mouth in circle shapes. The movement looks so sexy and appealing, you've got to love it.

Shun rolls his eyes and hits his chest. "Shit, that's strong ya-nah, eya bun this."

Brenda reaches for the spliff and puts her feet on the floor. Before she puts the joint to her lips, Shun lights the other one.

Boom! The room disappears into a thick cloud of smoke.

Brenda awkwardly puffs on the spliff and Shun notices. "Oi, cuz, what you doing? You're not buning right."

Shun extends his hand. "Oi, pass it here." He puts the joint to his lips. "Oh shit, you bum sucked the spliff."

He pulls on it hard and continues to draw in air through his mouth until he traps the smoke in his body. He swallows down some poison then blows out. Nothing flows.

"That's how you bun weed, you get me, cuzzy? Now bun it."

Brenda's first attempt leaves her choking and coughing. She tries again: one breath, two, three and four. Shun hands her the alcohol and she quickly takes a gulp then releases air; nothing flows, her body becomes light as a feather. She slouches back against the wall. Shun begins laughing. "Yes, cuz, you buzzing now, yeah."

Brenda nods then closes her eyes. She can't get out

of her mind how cheesy and sick the drugs man looked. He was fat, grotesquely fat, and his name was Obese. Pale, six foot two, thirty-two stones, with long brown greased back hair and flab jiggling off every part of his body. Some people called him, 'The fat, blue-eyed devil,' because he supplied the ghetto with poisonous drugs that destroyed people's minds and bodies.

He would argue, *'I'm just a mere businessman trading a wanted value without force, coercion or fraud and it's not my fault it's also poisonous and destructive and against the governments, at the moment, political agenda laws. I'm not selling it to create death; I'm doing it to make some bread.'*

Brenda blinks open her eyes to consider what Shun is saying to her. "Oi, Brenda, do you 'member when we were young and we had that dry sex?" He laughs to himself. "I didn't even put it in ya-nah."

Brenda doesn't answer as she lies on the bed stretched out looking at the ceiling. Her mind is still spinning as the room falls silent.

Shun's hand moves onto her leg. It moves higher and higher until it reaches the top of her thighs. Nothing is going to interrupt what's about to go down.

Shun pulls off his cousin's jacket, then the white vest underneath, exposing a black bra. He edges down the tight jeans, bringing with it Brenda's knickers. He mounts her... and releases his semen.

Chapter Thirty-Five

THE TIME IS WELL after 4 a.m. the following morning when Brenda arrives home. Before she enters the house, her thoughts flip back to when Shun had penetrated her. The penetration triggered off electricity that ran around her stomach. Brenda's nipples stiffen at the thought. She clutches her stomach as the electric feeling runs through her again. It feels different this time – it makes her feel grown-up spiritually, and brings her to a new understanding – that maybe she doesn't need money to receive happiness and that sweet sex is the answer.

With a wide grin, Brenda pushes open the front door slowly, so it won't creak too loud. Before she can close the door, Fasard is standing behind her. The years of bullshit and partying have been harsh on Fasard. Her once baby soft features are long gone and in their place is a face full of graters – missing back teeth with a few yellow ones in the front. Her arse and tits have also vanished.

"What the rass you done with my money?" Fasard's

voice is sharp and full of venom. It makes Brenda jump with fear as she spins around.

"Bitch, I asked you what you done with my pussyclart money?" continues Fasard, pointing her crooked finger at Brenda's face.

Brenda sucks air into her nose. "Ah, mum, man, why don't you go back to bed, man," she says in the most patronising voice she could manage.

"Hey, pickney, me and you ain't size ya-nah, don't renk yourself with me you know."

Brenda explodes into anger. "How you mean don't renk myself with you. You ain't been no mum to me, and yes, what? I took your money, what?! You ain't no mum to me, you ain't no mum. You don't give me shit or buy me shit. You act like I owe you something. I didn't ask to be born into this sickness, yeah?"

Tears fall from Brenda's eyes. Her frustration with the sickness in this world, in her life, makes her feel like killing, when all she wants is happiness; something she deserves. She looks her mother up and down cuts her eye, sucks on her teeth and begins to walk towards the kitchen.

With one swift motion, Brenda feels a backhand lash across her nose. Her immediate reaction leaves fingernail marks on her mother's face.

Fasard screams loudly, "Ah, you, bitch." She grabs her daughter's neck. The women tumble to the floor, rolling over on each other. Fasard's strength gives way and Brenda takes the advantage and pins her mother solidly to the floor. Fasard struggles, but it's no use.

"Mum, you listenin'?" Brenda's voice reveals

intense emotion. "I'm only gonna tell you this once. Don't ever put your hands on me again or…" Brenda pauses as tears run down her face. She wants to tell her mother that she would kill her but can't bring herself to say the deeply felt words. Brenda nudges her mother into the carpet then gets off her, leaving Fasard motionless and deflated after the first defeat at the hands of her daughter. She feels old and tired and her bones ache with a dull continuous pain as she watches Brenda walk off into the kitchen. An evil smirk spreads across Fasard's face. She wants revenge; she needs revenge.

Chapter Thirty-Six

BRENDA TURNS ON two fires under the pots. She removes a lid from one of them and catches a little water in the base of it to sprinkle water over the rice. Before she can replace the lid, a feeling of fear shudders down her spine.

"Ay, put down my rass pot lid," says Fasard in the most confident voice she can manage. Brenda lets the lid drop with a clang and turns around.

"I never cook no food for you... yeah. So just turn off them fires," Fasard stretches around Brenda, attempting to turn off the cooker.

"Leave them!" Brenda hits her mum's arms away from the knobs. Fasard responds with all the power she has left in her body and hurls Brenda onto the cooker. The pots fall to the floor. Brenda screams and lunges at her mother. Fasard swings around, snatches up a knife and plunges it into Brenda. Brenda halts with shock, not knowing whether to cry or run. Fasard throws the knife into the sink.

"You see? Like dats what you get, you little bitch.

You must honour and love your mother, yeah, and your days will be long upon this earth." Brenda doesn't reply. Fasard brushes past her and begins turning off the knobs while rambling on.

"Cha, you must tink say me and you are size. I brought you into this world and I will take you out. You hear that, bitch?"

Fasard's last few ramblings fall on deaf ears. Brenda is already out the front door. She shuts it with a bang, making Fasard realize she's talking to herself.

Chapter Thirty-Seven

THE EARLY MORNING AIR is fresh as it hits Brenda's face. She runs with panic and confusion. Thoughts of killing her mother are so strong she knows she would do it.

'Fuck you, about honour and love thy mother. I'm meant to honour you, no matter what you do. Nah, fuck that,' she says to herself while slowing down to a fast walk.

Deep questions penetrate her mind. *'Do I really have to honour and love my mother no matter what she does to me? But if I don't, why would she lie? Could it be for control? What happens if I don't love and honour her? She says my days will be short upon this earth, which sounds good to me.'* Brenda begins to sense the dishonesties and manipulated truths her mother has hidden behind to cover up her deceptions and destructions.

She feels powerless and lost and her insides are all twisted up. She ponders why the world is this way. *'Who made it this way? What can change it? Who will change it? Why hasn't it changed already? What are the answers? Can a poverty-driven person like me discover them? Are they hidden or are they told with misguided truths?'*

Brenda sniffles, dries her tears, then picks up her pace down the empty roads and streets.

Chapter Thirty-Eight

THE ENTRANCE TO THE housing block Brenda is walking through is filled with turned-over bins with rubbish scattered everywhere and graffiti on the walls. Even though the sun is rising, parts of the housing estate are in darkness. In these parts, Brenda holds her breath. Just a few more blocks and she'll be out of the estate and on Shun's road.

She has stopped bleeding from her injuries but she is still in pain. Looking up ahead, she can see a small group of people at the end of the last block. It isn't unusual to see people standing and talking and heading nowhere in the early morning hours on a housing estate. She gets closer and realises that one of them is Shun. He sees her.

"Hold on my yout, hold on," he says without respect to the youth that is asking him for a spliff. He steps out of the small huddle of bodies towards his cousin.

The members of the group focus their attention on Shun and Brenda. They watch Shun's arms fly up in the air, seeming to be asking, 'How? Why? When?' As the couple walk off to an alleyway that circles onto Shun's road, one member of the group mentions, "You know he's sexing his cousin doh, innit?"

Chapter Thirty-Nine

SHUN IS JOLTED OUT of his sleep holding his cousin in his meaty arms. The time reads 10 a.m. on the kettle he peeled the weekend before. The watch isn't even that heavy, but it has bling-bling within the dials, so it's good enough to rock.

His day of hustle will be starting in the next hour, but he has one problem – what to do with Brenda.

Shun slides his arm from underneath Brenda's neck. He reaches for a half a spliff on the windowsill, sparks it and beats his chest as the smoke hurts his throat and lungs. He coughs up phlegm and spits it into a beer bottle by the side of his bed.

Brenda opens her eyes and smiles, feeling the answer to her problems is sweet sex, because all of the pent-up emotions from last night have disappeared leaving her feeling relaxed and happy.

Shun looks at her with serious eyes. "So what you gonna do?"

"Err, do what?" Replies Brenda.

"Today, innit, what you gonna do today? Because

you know I'm going out there. On a move, you get me?"

Brenda thinks for a moment… she never wants to leave Shun's side. "But, like, can't I come with you?"

Shun thinks for a second… "Boy, I don't know about dat you know." He thinks for another second. *Yeah, the female company might be good, plus it would be a good deterrent to have a girl in the car just in case the boy-dem start some shit.*

"Ah, go on. Please, man, don't be like that."

Shun shakes his head. "Boy, I don't really know, you know, man? 'Cause on road is no joke, you over? People can die outside."

"I know dat. I'm not scared of dat, I just wanna be with you, innit? So what, you gonna let me roll?"

Shun smiles, "Alright, you listenin'? Whatever I tell you to do, you gotta do. No long ting."

Brenda nods her head and bites down on her bottom lip. Shun gets off the bed and sparks the spliff again.

Brenda swallows some spit, then stutters, "But, but these clothes I've got on are dirty. I can't wear them."

"Nah, don't watch dat. You're rolling with me now. I'm gonna get you some new shit, eya bun dis."

Shun hands over the spliff, picks up his phone and exits the room, leaving Brenda to crush her lungs.

Chapter Forty

THE GREY HOUSING BLOCKS are quiet. Shun jumps out of the ride with his phone stuck to his ear and runs over a grassed area and into one of the housing blocks, leaving Brenda in the car.

Forty-five minutes pass before Shun finally exits the building. He is holding a blue plastic bag and still talking on his phone. When he enters the car he throws the bag on the back seat, starts the engine and ends his call.

Brenda's loved-up eyes widen. "What's that in the bag?"

"Just cool, man."

"Nah, I just… "

Shun cuts in, "Nah, Bee, you listening? The less you know the better, but you need to be serious, you need to put on your game face, you get me?"

"Yeah, minor, minor, I'm gonna do dat."

"Are you sure?"

Brenda gives a reassuring nod.

"Because when we get to the move, it ain't no back down ting, you over?" Shun looks deep into his cousin's eyes, making sure that duty and fear will influence her to take the action he wants her to take.

"Okay, you listenin'? We have to go to your house. You need some make-up, a short skirt and a low top."

"But I thought you said you're gonna buy…"

Shun cuts in. "What did I tell you back at the yard, huh?"

Brenda falls silent. Shun sucks his teeth and takes off.

Chapter Forty-One

BRENDA HAS BUTTERFLIES as Shun pulls into her housing block. He parks the car and waits for her. She moves slowly, then picks up pace until she reaches her landing.

Brenda is locked out, but she has a way of getting in without a key. She picks up a piece of scrap wood outside the bin chute, puts her arm and the stick of wood through the letterbox and aims at the handle of the latch inside. After a few moments, Brenda catches it and the door springs open.

Her nerves are tingling all over her body as she steps into the house without closing the door behind her and moves quickly to her bedroom.

Although all her other clothes are dirty, she desperately doesn't want to disappoint her cousin and right about now the only place Brenda can find clean clothes is in her mother's room. She looks at the time: 12:30 p.m. Her mum will still be asleep for sure.

Brenda creeps towards Fasard's room. Inside it is dark from a woollen curtain blocking out the cold sun.

Brenda nudges the door open, peeps in, and can't believe her eyes– her mother isn't there. Ever since Brenda could remember, her mum never rose until late evening. Brenda doesn't waste any more time thinking why, how, when; she switches on the bedroom light and grabs what she needs.

Chapter Forty-Two

SHUN IS TALKING on his phone as Brenda comes wobbling towards the car. She's wearing her mother's jeans suit, which exposes her shoulders, arms, belly and most of her legs. The heels on her feet make her close to five foot nine. The make-up on her face ages her ten years. She gets into the car all sexy like, and places a big plastic bag between her legs and a hand-bag on her lap.

"I'm ready," she says, turning her face towards Shun.

Shun ends the call and asks, "Where you get all that shit from?"

"That's my business, innit?" replies Brenda in a whisper.

"Ter, 'old on, what, ay don't go like your bad ya-nah." Brenda swallows nervously. Shun smirks. "Anyway, you look good doh." He runs his eyes over her. "What, you ready to roll?" If she wasn't Shun didn't care – he would result to force if he had to.

Shun stretches over the car seat for the blue plastic

bag, opens it and takes out a chequebook and card, handing it to Brenda.

"Eya, take this bun and cheese and put it in your bag." He pauses in thought. "Yeah, hold Betsy Sue as well." Shun places the wrapped up gun into Brenda's bag. Brenda doesn't argue; she doesn't know what Betsy Sue is, all she knows about is the excitement she is feeling.

Shun starts the car and moves off while explaining the deal with the chequebook and card.

Chapter Forty-Three

SHUN STOPS THE CAR outside the destination; his phone is once again glued to his ear. Brenda's heart is beating and her palms are sweating. Shun had explained she would go into the Bureau De Change with the chequebook and credit card, hand them over to the cashier with a small parcel inside the crease of the chequebook.

Brenda steps out of the car with her heart beating a little faster, but her steps are strong. Looking at her, she appears cool as a breeze; relaxed, but not too relaxed.

Her mind goes over the instructions Shun gave her. One: hand over the bun and cheese. Two: sign the slip of paper that the cashier gives you. Three: wait for the money. Four: recount the money. Five: take the bun and cheese, then leave.

Brenda loses her nerve but it's too late – the cashier sees her. His voice booms through the microphone behind the three-inch window.

"Can I help you, madam," he says, with eyes that look as if he's expecting her.

Brenda doesn't answer as she walks into the empty shop-front towards the counter. She feels relaxed seeing that the shop is empty. It's just her and the soft-featured male. His face looks trustworthy, but something about him isn't right. Brenda has no time to think what it is. She hands over the things.

The cashier is more interested in the chequebook than handing over the cash slip. He fumbles through it then finds what he wants. He reaches below his desk and pushes out a white slip of paper. Brenda quickly signs it and pushes it back. The cashier reaches under his desk. This time he comes up with a bundle of funny-looking money. Brenda's heart nearly stops.

He counts the notes twice then slips it through. Brenda forgets what to do next. Her head is dizzy as she stutters, "Umm, umm, is that it?"

The cashier raises his eyebrows to the ceiling and slides the bun and cheese through, then says with nervous eyes and a smile. "Yes, miss, thank you, please come again."

Brenda doesn't argue. She turns and disappears with the money and the bun and cheese safely in her bag.

Chapter Forty-Four

SHUN IS STILL talking on his phone as Brenda appears from around the corner with a smile spread across her face. She jumps in and for a few seconds she doesn't talk as she breathes in and out deeply.

Shun looks at her as if concerned for her welfare. He ends the call. "What, are you all right?"

Brenda swallows. "Yeah," she says with a nod.

"So what, you got the papers, yeah?"

"Yeah," Brenda says again and dips into her handbag. She removes the bundle of funny money and gives it to Shun.

"Rah, how much he give you?"

"Umm," Brenda scratches her head. She couldn't remember the total.

Shun begins flicking out each note, counting them as quick as he flicks them.

"How much is there?" enquires Brenda.

"Plenty."

"How much is plenty?"

"Just cool, man, there's enough."

"What type of money is that anyway, it looks funny?"

"Foreign money."

Panic comes over Brenda's face. She thought the funny-looking money was a new type that the county had just brought in.

"But we can't use them over here?"

"I told you, just cool, man. I'm gonna deal wid it, you get me?"

Shun is pissed that the crack-head cashier gave him foreign notes, but money's money. Shun is glad that the transaction went down smoothly. He can now pay for Betsy Sue and the bun and cheese he got on tick from an older head who is always willing to help the young-sters cause destruction.

Chapter Forty-Five

SHUN PULLS UP OUTSIDE a bank across town. The female bank manager is a very good friend of his and she will spin the funny money into his currency, with no questions asked.

Shun's phone rings. He answers it and in the same breath tells Brenda to wait in the car. Brenda is tired and frustrated. "Where you going, man?" she says, vexed.

"Just cool, man. Wait here, man." Shun jumps out of the car as Brenda sucks on her teeth.

Moments later Shun returns without the phone stuck to his ear. He starts the car and takes off.

"Where we going now?" demands Brenda.

"How you love ask so much question?"

"Yeah, but where're we going?"

Shun sucks on his teeth. "What did I tell you? Stop ask bomboclart question, man."

"Yeah, like I'm hungry doh, innit."

"Yeah, well we ain't dun rolling yet. So just cool, man."

Shun answers his phone and looks over at Brenda's screwed-up face, planning to spite her. He decides to give her a cut from the money after he uses her for the next move, which is a bit riskier than the last.

On the way, Shun pulls into a fast food drive-in, and breaks down the next move. Brenda doesn't argue. The next move is set.

Chapter Forty-Six

BRENDA'S BELLY IS FULL. Shun gives her a spliff.

"Now remember what I said, yeah, just knock the door and ask for Massif. When it opens up, all you have to do is move out of the way."

"Yeah, yeah." Brenda is nervous but willing.

They get out of the car and go up to the sixth floor. Shun points out the door. Brenda moves towards it while Shun hides in a blind spot and waits.

The door opens and Shun rushes forward, bouncing Brenda out of the way. He doesn't recognise the male. The male isn't Massif. Massif is big-boned and tall, and this male is small-boned and short, as if the skin of a grown-up was wrapped around the body of a child.

"Where the rass is, Massif?"

The small male speaks in a deep, gravelly voice, "Who's, Massif?"

"Ay listen, don't take man for nah fool, ya-nah. I'll buss face wid su'um, ya-nah."

The little man shows no fear, as if he expected what is happening and has fully prepared for it.

Shun pushes him in the chest. The little man tries to firm it and pushes back, but it's no use. Shun walks past him and moves down the hallway.

"Oi, stop!" This is an order. Shun spins around. What happens next seems to happen in slow motion. The little man is pointing a gun and he fires. On reflex, Shun jumps back, and the bullet leaves its heat on his leg and flies out the other side of his tracksuit bottoms.

The little man squeezes again, but this time nothing comes out – the gun sticks. Fear enters the little man's eyes. Betsy Sue is staring at him. Shun squeezes and peppers the little man twice. He falls to the floor as Shun feels the backfire of the gunpowder stain his skin.

Chapter Forty-Seven

FROM OUTSIDE THE DOOR, the first gunshot sounds like a bomb. Brenda closes her eyes, holds her stomach and runs towards the lift. The second shot makes her scream. Tears come to her eyes. She pushes the lift button frantically. The third shot makes her forget about the lift. She takes off and runs for the emergency stairs. One flight, two flights, three flights – she stops. Tremendous guilt consumes her. She is abandoning the one she loves – and she can't do it. The implicit rules of the world she entered when she agreed to roll were 'ride or die' – that's how it goes down. No time for half-way steppers who think destruction or death is a long way off. It's just around the corner. It could happen on your first move or the next hundred and fifty moves. What's certain is that it will happen.

Brenda wipes away her tears. The only thing she really has to lose is her life and deep down, she doesn't value it. Brenda turns and goes back to her loved one.

She moves slowly towards the door, with her heart

beating hard. The thought of the pain behind dying still scares her. She jumps back and nearly screams as a figure runs through the open door. She controls herself when she realises it's Shun. He grabs her arm with his free hand and pulls her along the hallway and back down the escape stairs.

Chapter Forty-Eight

THE COUPLE BURST out of the downstairs door. Shun slows them down, trying to avoid looking bait. There is no need. If any neighbours saw or heard anything, they wouldn't get involved until any more risk of trouble had gone. As for police, they never patrolled that part of the ends. They blamed it on lack of manpower due to decreasing budgets.

"Shun, what happen man, what happen?"

Shun doesn't reply. His eyes are spinning wildly around. From the moment he blazed the little man, his mind went into overdrive.

The first thing was to move through the house, looking for anybody else, ready to blaze them too. Nobody was in, but there were two stacks: one was money, the other was cocaine. Shun immediately bagged up the papers and the whites then quickly looked for anything else to cop. On the way out, he ripped the iced-out kettle off the little man's wrist. He stopped outside the bathroom. An idea came to him. He picked up a towel, removed the heat from his waist, wiped it clean and dashed it on the floor. He thought it would be a good way to end one lead the police would have: the hunt for the murder weapon.

He looked back on the destruction he was leaving. The place was silent. Not a thing moved, which gave him a false sense of power. He jumped through the door, as if he was too bad for the world.

He knew this moment had changed his game forever. He would stop shotting rocks on the block and start peeling top shotters. But right about now, he has to get away.

He reaches the car, nudges Brenda towards the passenger side and tells her to get in.

'From now on,' Shun tells himself, 'I'm not watching no face; everyone will get robbed, pussy fi lay down.'

Chapter Forty-Nine

SHUN PULLS UP in a back street ten miles away from the murder scene. The car is silent except for the deep bass and drumbeats from the speakers.

Shun turns down the noise. "Oi, Bee, you listening, yeah? Take this money here and go and buy me a pair of gloves and stop at the corner shop and buy some washing-up liquid or su'um, yeah?"

Brenda exits the car. In the meantime, Shun sorts out the money. Two gees for the older head and two and a half for Brenda. She done well and he thought she deserved it. The rest of the papers he hides in different parts of his clothing. The cocaine he puts on the back seat. He thinks about plugging it, but why go through that pain?

Brenda returns. Shun takes the bag and puts the gloves on.

"Come we go," he orders.

"Go where?"

Shun gives Brenda a look and she knows what it means: don't ask questions.

She pauses before leaving the car, wanting to con-front Shun. The day is getting later and later and there will be no time to buy anything, she thinks.

"Oi, Bee, come on man, get out the car man." This time Brenda slams the door and follows.

Chapter Fifty

SHUN LEADS BRENDA into a café – one that only sells greasy food. He tells her to sit in a booth while he goes to scrub the gunpowder off his hand. A slim, smiling waiter with slicked back hair steps over to Brenda's booth with a pen and white pad.

"Order?"

"Sorry?" says Brenda, looking up from the table.

"Order, take your order please?"

"Oh, my order." Brenda isn't hungry – she just wants to leave so she makes an excuse. "I'm on a diet and you sell nothing but greasy, fattening food."

"Fatty food good for you, make you lose weight, like in book."

Brenda looks at the waiter as if he is mad. She has never heard of carbohydrate poisoning before.

"Nah, nah, nah. Just bring me a coke, man." Brenda waves the smiling waiter away as if he is an imbecile.

Shun returns from the restroom talking on his phone and still wearing the gloves, his hands are still patched in places from the gunpowder.

Brenda gets up. "Yeah, we off now, yeah?"

Shun waves her down. "Nah, sit down." He ends the call and slides the phone on the table, "We're not going yet."

They both sit down. Shun's hands are busy underneath the table shuffling money. Without looking up at Brenda, he says, "What, did you order su'um?"

"Nah, just a can of coke. You know the idiot man try say fatty food is good for you."

"Yeah," Shun swallows, "eya, see if this is good for you." He throws a small stack of money on the table in the empty café.

Brenda's eyes widen. "Is that for me?"

"Why, you don't want it?"

"Course I do." Brenda grabs the money, "How much is here?"

"Two and half gees, standard."

That little girl excitement fills Brenda's eyes again.

"I can't believe it." She says, putting the money in her bag and giving Shun a hug and a kiss.

Shun drives her up-town for some late night shopping followed by some sweet loving. With these new money and sweet sex experiences, she feels consumed by another realm of happiness. Although it ends within a few hours, Brenda plans on getting more where it came from as she becomes hooked on sweet sex and the hype of the paper chase.

Chapter Fifty-One

THE APRIL SHOWERS had stopped falling five months ago and it is now the second week of a brand new school term.

Shun runs out of a dilapidated house holding his waist and jumps into his car.

"Start the car, start the car."

Brenda puts the car into gear. A man with a vexed face comes dashing out of the house. Brenda takes off. Shun winds down the window and shouts, "Hey, pussyhole, go suck your, muddar."

The vexed man responds. He aims and buses off shots but misses.

Brenda swerves the car to the left, then right, then pulls it under control. She takes the corner in third gear, leaving behind her the screeching sounds of the tyres and the man shouting. "Watch-watch, pussyhole, watch."

Brenda looks at Shun's face. A lump is rising on his forehead just above his eyebrow.

"Um, babes, you're getting a coco on your fore-head."

"Ah, it ain't nuffing." Begins Shun, making it known that it's just part of the grime. 'It's nuffing.'

"Them pussyholes try rush, man, innit, before I could even pull out my stick, rudeboy. They were all over me. I sparked out two of dem, rudeboy, my stick all drop on the floor. I had to blow, rudeboy."

Brenda is nodding her head listening to the story of another risky escape. They always excite her; she does-n't even mind anymore that Shun talks to her like she's one of the mans-dem, by calling her rudeboy.

"Hey, rudeboy, it's all good doh, man still got the loot. You listening?"

Shun pulls out the money from down his jeans.

"Oi, stop at this shop here."

Brenda parks the car in front of an off-licence. Shun jumps out and walks past a drunk standing outside. The drunk catches Brenda's eye. His hair and beard are picky and his clothes are ragged and smelly. His face and hands are swollen. Dirt grows thick underneath his fingernails. He holds onto his beer can tightly, even though it seems he is sleeping standing up. His knees move slowly towards the ground. Before he drops, he quickly jerks himself up, still gripping the beer can tightly, with his eyes shut. Up and down he goes like a puppet on a string.

Shun steps out of the shop with his phone pressed to his ear. The drunk must have felt someone staring at him, and he raises his head from the ground, his grill comes into view. Shun doesn't recognise him, but

Brenda does. She turns her face as a tear comes to her eye.

Shun gets in the car, moves the phone away from his mouth and says to Brenda,

"Oi, did you see that, bum?" He points at the drunk and puts the phone back to his mouth for a few seconds, then removes it. "He's rocked," continues Shun as he begins to laugh. "Come, Bee, let's go."

Shun puts the phone back to his mouth and resumes the conversation with the person on the other end.

Brenda takes one last look at her father bopping up and down, puts the car into gear and takes off.

Chapter Fifty-Two

DEEP DOWN WITHIN, the voice of honesty speaks to Brenda. She feels like crying and asking how this has happened to her father. *Is it because this world guarantees destruction for everyone and then finally, death? Is there no difference between being on your sick bed dying of natural causes or standing outside an off-licence poisoning your blood and dying slowly? At the end of the day, when you're dead you're dead. It doesn't matter what you died from your life is gone. The only hope is living on beyond, and you can't even rely on that.*

Brenda's thoughts make her feel doomed. She is worried how much longer she has left until her happiness turns to destruction.

Shun offers her a couple of pulls on his spliff. The weed smoke represses the worrying thoughts for a while. She carries on driving smoothly towards Shun's yard while other thoughts enter her mind. Maybe she'll be lucky and the happiness with Shun will last forever. She says a silent prayer as she pulls the car up to the curb. Seeing Shun's front door makes her feel elated. Brenda smiles within, as it's time to be submerged within her loved one's private universe.

Brenda and Shun exit the car and walk towards Shun's house. Brenda truly loves this part of the day. She smiles, hoping that her prayer will be answered and this happiness will never end.

Chapter Fifty-Three

THE GOVERNMENT BUILDING is old and gloomy-looking; This one has long windows, ones that you can't see into and can hardly see out of. It's early morning outside but inside, if trapped in an office on the third floor, it could be the middle of the night – you wouldn't know the difference. Bodies walk in and out of the building. The ones leaving look relieved. The ones entering look doomed, except for one – Miss Sandra Secret. She walks tall and confident, her whole muscler physique moving smoothly beneath her tailored skirt-suit.

Miss Secret enters the lift and takes it to the third floor, leaving her scent behind in the reception and lift. She walks towards the corner office. The outside door reads, "Sally McNeal, Senior Social Worker."

Sandra enters and is greeted with a wide smile from Ms McNeal, a small woman with caring features and soft brown eyes.

"Please take a seat."

With a smile, Sandra sits down with eyes and ears

fixed on Ms McNeal's every move and sound.

Ms McNeal shuffles some papers and places them in front of her, then begins to speak in a high-pitched middle-class tone. "Would you like a cup of coffee, Miss Secret?"

"No, thank you," replies Sandra in a tone suggesting 'let's get on with business'.

Ms McNeal clears her throat. "Okay, this first case involves a child by the name of..." She glances down quickly. "Oh yes, Brenda Rote. The education authorities have notified us that she has been absent from school for the last two terms."

Ms McNeal slides the folder across. "As you can see, she is still only twelve years old, so they have instructed us to investigate her home life."

Sandra closes the dossier. "I see there has been trouble with her attendance in the past. The first time was when she was six. These records show she has missed three years of schooling. Then a further four terms between the ages of ten and eleven."

Ms McNeal has a nervous twitch that appears under stress. She tries to control it by telling herself that she's the senior authority here. Twitch, twitch. It's no use – Sandra has genuine power.

"So, what measures were taken to prevent this problem in the past?" continues Sandra.

Ms McNeal almost stutters, "None. I believe due to departmental dissemination." This just means the department responsible for truancy had its files mixed up with other files. Basically, Brenda's file was lost. Ms McNeal picks up her cup of poison and sips. Her twitch stops as she calmly instructs Sandra. "So what I would want, Ms Secret, is for you to make our department look good with this case. You will get all the help you need."

Sandra knows the deal. She gives a nod and a smile, picks up the dossier, politely excuses herself and leaves.

Chapter Fifty-Four

ON HER WAY OVER to Brenda's, Sandra was dwelling on all the dishonesty, the lies and the scape-goating from the higher authorities: the arbitrary procedures and red tape that told you when to move and when not to. Even if you suspected a child was being abused but couldn't prove it, you had to go by the book. Usually this meant it was too late – either the child had run away or was found dead.

Sandra shakes her head in disgust. She knows that a case like this could be her last case. She must tread careful or they will sacrifice her.

Sandra pulls up at Brenda's housing block. She glances at the door number on the folder and puts it back in her bag. She takes out her ID card and steps out of the car.

She takes the grey concrete stairs to the second floor. She walks down the landing to the last door on the right. The paint on the door is peeling, the letterbox is hanging off, black soot covers the outside window frames and the doorstep has a dried paint stain on it.

Sandra presses the dirt-covered doorbell; it doesn't work, so she bangs on the door. Moments later, it opens.

Chapter Fifty-Five

FASARD'S EYES ARE half-open, her hair is all messed up and her mouth unwashed. She's wearing what she slept in: a vest exposing the top of her sagging breasts, and baggy leggings that cover the top half of the rail-road stretch marks running down her cellulite backside.

"Yes, what is it?"

Fasard always spoke bluntly whenever opening the door to a police-like bang.

"Are you, Ms Fasard Rote?"

"Why, what do you want?" replies Fasard, as she wipes matter from the corners of her eyes.

Sandra points to her ID, "I'm with the Social Service, my name is Sandra Secret," she states.

Fasard's attitude changes. "Oh, why didn't you say. Oh yes, I'm Missus Rote." Fasard's heart is beating hard; she thinks Brenda somehow got to the boy-dem and told them what she had done.

"That's good. So are you aware that your daughter has been absent from school since the start of last term and for the first two weeks of this new term?"

Fasard places her hand on her hip and adopts a concerned expression. "No, I didn't." Fasard doesn't say anything else as she tries to figure out what Sandra is leading to.

"Well, I'm here to investigate Brenda's home life, to see if there are any problems or reasons why she isn't attending school."

Fasard's heart skips a beat, but she plays it cool.

"Oh, everything is fine here. I send her to school every morning, but you know these kids – bunking off is like a trend."

Sandra smiles. "I see. So did you send her to school this morning?"

Fasard folds her arms then unfolds them. "Yeah, I did. I sent her to school." Fasard bites down on her thumbnail then rubs the corner of her mouth. She's fiending for a fag, and wondering if Sandra has spotted her lying.

Sandra puts her ID back into her purse.

"Okay, because this is a very serious matter, if you can spare a few moments I would like to ask you a few more questions inside."

Fasard hesitates, then releases the door. Her nerves are still jangled, but at least she can now get that fag.

Sandra steps inside and isn't surprised that Fasard's house is no different from those of other unproductive individuals who receive free housing from the government. Wallpaper mildewing and peeling from the wall, dirt-covered floorboards that creak beneath her feet and clothes hanging from the staircase.

As the door closes behind Sandra, the frowzy scent of the house hits her in the face.

Chapter Fifty-Six

EARLY THE NEXT MORNING, Shun is taking Brenda on another moneymaking move. Sandra has another day of investigations. After leaving Brenda's house the day before, she had called the school to get an appointment to see the Head. She is now on her way over.

Brenda is on her way to some streets she hasn't seen before. She sits silently in the front passenger seat. Shun's driving; speeding down the motorway, music blazing. Three thugs sit squashed in the back seat; the one in the middle speaks.

"Oi, Shun, you listening? If su'um goes nuts, it's every man for himself, ya-nah?"

"Shut up, man. Stop washing your mouth, man. Shut up man. Nuffing ain't gonna go wrong. And stop watching my cousin – she rolls wid me, man, are you stupid?"

The thug sucks on his teeth, and falls back into the seat. He says something to the other two thugs. Shun ignores him and turns to Brenda.

"Oi, Bee." He begins in a voice that only Brenda can hear. "Don't watch them idiots, yeah. Oi, you remember what I told you – if the boy-dem ever suck onto you, don't tell them nuffing. Nuffing. You listenin'? 'Cause they can't do you nuffing, so just do what I said, give fake name and age. Wors' ways your under age, first offence."

Shun pulls off the motorway and Brenda tries to memorise the date of birth and name she plans to use, wors' ways.

Chapter Fifty-Seven

SANDRA STOPS HER car outside Brenda's school. She takes a moment to wonder how the only thing missing from the twelve-foot high fence that surrounds the school is barbwire. Then it would be no different from a minimum security prison.

What is the fence for? Protection for the children? It can't be – the gate is open. Sandra pushes it and walks straight in. She strides down the wide stone staircase towards the school building.

The playground is silent. You can't tell if there is life in the building – the school seems closed.

Sandra enters the foyer – it's empty, no receptionist. She looks up at the big school clock on the wall and sees she's five minutes early. Sandra takes a seat on a chair provided and waits patiently.

"Let me go! Let me go!" are the screams coming down the hallway. Sandra stands up.

"Calm down, calm down."

"Nah-nah, I don't care, yeah, I don't care."

As the teacher and pupil reach the foyer, the pupil

shrugs off the teacher's grip.

"Just let me go, yeah." He walks up to the main doors, huffing and puffing, stops, and spins around.

"Please, Savant, come and sit down." Savant huffs and spins back towards the door. The teacher rubs his forehead, then notices Sandra.

"I'm sorry, can I help?"

"Yes. I am here to see the Headmaster, Mr. Bowden.

The teacher raises his eyebrows. "Okay, one moment." He takes a last, pissed-off look at Savant, then turns and walks to the Head's office. Just before he enters, he looks back at Sandra. "I'm sorry, who did you say you were?"

Sandra looks back at him as if to say I didn't.

"I'm from the Social Services," she says with a smile as the teacher disappears into the office.

Chapter Fifty-Eight

SANDRA LOOKS OVER AT the youth as he huffs and paces. She makes eye contact and offers him a stick of sugar-free gum. He stops pacing.

"You know, I hated teachers too," she says.

The youth's eyes show interest.

"I didn't even finish school because of them, and most lessons were mad boring." The youth smiles. He takes the gum and sits down.

"So if you didn't finish school, how come you got a good job now?"

"I had to go back to school, innit, when I was older. But when I did I didn't hate it so much, because I wasn't being forced to learn, I wanted to learn, you get me?" Sandra slips into ghetto slang and, looking younger than her age, makes the youth feel comfortable.

"Yeah, you know dat my teacher try force me to read in front of the class, yeah, and I didn't want to, yeah, so she try give me detention, yeah, so I told her to fuck off den, innit."

"Yeah, I hear that, your name's, Savant, innit?"

Savant nods his head.

"Yeah, I had a teacher like that when I was in school too, but it wasn't because I couldn't read. I had a stutter and I was ashamed of it. I ended up hating the teachers and lost interest in the lessons, so I bunked off school more and more, until I never went back."

Sandra stops to take note if the youth is listening. He's deep in thought.

"Then when I finally went back, yeah, when I was older, and I was told to read, I simply got up and forced the words out. I told the teacher about my stutter and that I preferred not to read. And you know what? I was never asked to read again. Instead I was sent to a speech class."

The Headmaster's door opens. "What I'm trying to say is being honest solved my problem – and any other problem that could have come up, you get me?"

Savant nods his head and Sandra gives him a wink.

"Keep your head up," she says, then walks into the office.

She spends the next two hours hearing nothing but bad reports about Brenda and how the level of her reading and writing are well below average.

Chapter Fifty-Nine

THE CAR IS UP on the pavement and Brenda is at the steering wheel. Four males are fleeing from the car and the one in front is Shun. All around sirens are screaming, adding to the confusion.

"ARMED POLICE, DON'T MOVE!"

Brenda freezes as tears fall to her cheek.

The fed with the biggest chest shouts to his crew, "Stand down!"

He orders Brenda out of the car. She gets out slowly and the fed approaches her and gives her a quick pat down. A local police van pulls up and unarmed police takes over from the armed feds. Brenda wipes away the tears and begins to recall her fake name and age as a friendly looking officer approaches her and unclips his handcuffs. "You're under arrest," he says, and leads her to the police van.

Brenda's mind is spinning – she can't remember the aliases and again the tears start to fall. Before she gets into the car, she looks up at the iron bird buzzing around in the sky. It already has the four runaways locked in its radar. There is no escape for them and eventually they're picked up one by one.

The officer at the nick's front desk asks Brenda four questions: name, age, DOB, and address. Brenda can't spell the name she gives, the age doesn't match with the DOB, and the address is hot. But that isn't the worst of her problems – the name and DOB are those of a wanted person.

The front desk officer shakes his head then sends her to one of the cold cells until morning, when the superior officer arrives.

Chapter Sixty

THE SUPERIOR OFFICER , with his over polished shoes, steps into his office. The duty officer enters before he can sit down.

"Good morning, sir. Here are today's cases."

He hands the Super a handful of official papers.

The Super sits down and puts on his glasses, which slide down to the tip of his nose. He begins to scan the charges on Brenda, Shun and the rest. He looks concerned.

"Who made the arrests?"

"Strong and Biggs."

"Where are they now?"

"In the holding rooms, sir."

"Are they ready to commence interviewing?"

"Yes sir, I believe so."

The Super looks down at the charge papers then back up again. He takes off his glasses.

"How many bodies have we got, apart from these?"

The officer answers sharply, "Sixteen, sir."

The Super looks pleased. "Okay. Tell Strong and

Biggs to begin with the girl, and no rough stuff – she could be the key to this case."

The Super hands the papers back to the duty officer.

"And make sure they keep me posted."

"Yes, sir." The duty officer spins on the heels of his unpolished shoes and heads for the cells.

Chapter Sixty-One

BRENDA'S HEAD IS pounding and her mouth is dry. The tears of fear have stopped falling and tears of disappointment are rolling down her cheeks. Her idea of the world destroying everything is proving right, but deep down she doesn't want to believe it because she's in love with the excitement and happiness that the grime provides. If only she could enjoy the happiness without the harsh consequences then it'll be all-good. Brenda laughs at that thought – she knows that she's trapped, because to be with Shun and experience those moments of happiness is to be with the grime and the harsh consequences it delivers. A spark of madness enters Brenda's confused mind. She wishes she has a belt so she could hang herself and be dead and gone.

Hearing the heavy bolt on the iron cell door sliding, she looks up and wipes the tears from her red, bloodshot eyes.

The little flap in the middle of the door opens and crystal clear blue eyes pierce through at her.

"Are you okay?" asks the duty officer.

Brenda moves off her back and onto her bottom, but she doesn't answer. The officer flips back the flap and, with a noisy clang, he pulls the second bolt and opens the door. "Come with me, please."

Brenda walks towards the door, wondering if it is night or day outside. She looks for a window as the officer leads her down the hallway to the interview room. On the way he tries to make conversation.

"So, is this your first time in trouble?"

Brenda was going to answer but sucks on her teeth instead.

The officer continues, "Well, I suppose this won't be your last." He doesn't expect a reply – he just grins and keeps walking.

Chapter Sixty-Two

THE INTERVIEW ROOM DOOR is open and Biggs and Strong are in conversation. They quickly end it with a laugh as Brenda and the officer appear.

"Here's the first body." The duty officer motions Brenda to a seat in front of a desk. The two officers walk out of the room with the duty officer and leave Brenda by herself.

Brenda sits there collecting her thoughts. She knows the first thing to do is to reveal her real name, age and address and then worry about the questions the boy-dem will fire at her.

The officers are about to re-enter the room. Brenda quickly tries to remember what happened exactly. All she knew was that they were going on a move. What the move was, she didn't know. Shun ordered her to sit in the car and get ready to drive, waiting for them to return. When they came back running and shouting, she drove off, and the next minute the boy-dem were chasing and ramming her off the road.

Brenda's thoughts cease as the officers enter the room moving with intimidation and puffing out their chests. They sit down and start the tape recorder. Brenda gives her real age, name and address. The tape recorder stops and the two officers look at each other, dumbfounded. They get up and slam the door. They abuse the duty officer for a bit then check the information with the relevant government bodies. They shout some more, then recheck. Somewhere down the line, Sandra receives notification.

Chapter Sixty-Three

SANDRA SITS CROSSED-LEGGED in the police waiting area on a red steel chair. When the call came through she made it to the out-of-town police station as quickly as she could.

Sandra has been waiting for over an hour but remains patiently seated like a prisoner on twenty-three hour bang up, waiting for that one hour of exercise.

The brown door on her left opens and Brenda appears in front of a policewoman. Sandra uncrosses her legs as the officer at the front desk motions to her. Sandra gets up and moves towards Brenda.

"Hi, Brenda." Brenda's name comes to her in an unfamiliar voice.

"Hi, my name is Sandra Secret. I'm your social worker."

Sandra extends her hand for a handshake and gives a nod to the policewoman that she will take it from there. Brenda pulls her hand back. "I don't know you!"

"I'm your social worker."

"Yeah, but I don't know you."

The policewoman steps back through the brown door.

"Now, please, young lady. This is your social worker – you have to go with her."

"I don't have to go with her. I don't know her. I'm not going with her."

"Oh yes you will, unless you want to go back to the cells."

Brenda sucks on her teeth. The fear of going back to the cell is enough. She leaves quietly with Sandra behind her.

Chapter Sixty-Four

BEFORE THEY REACH the car, Sandra asks, "Brenda, are you listenin'?" Brenda looks surprised by how Sandra's voice suddenly sounds street.

"What happened back there is what rules this world, you listenin'? Force and fraud is what it is. Obviously you didn't want to come with me, but you were forced to... under fraud."

Brenda doesn't speak, but her eyes are asking *'what's the fraud?'* Sandra asks the question for her.

"What is the fraud? Making you and others believe that they all care about your welfare and want you to grow up a decent, law-abiding citizen. But in all honesty most of them would rather you become a criminal because without criminals or making people into criminals they will lose most of their bogus jobs and controlling power over others."

Brenda's expression shows interest. "So how dey make us into criminals?"

"First, they create poverty. Then they choose a few harmful substances and make them illegal. This creates an opportunity to escape poverty, turning innocent, poverty-driven people into subjective criminals."

Sandra places her hand on Brenda's arm and they stop walking. She closes her eyes for a moment.

"Breaking free from the poverty trap is difficult, because the things it leads to puts excitement in your life. That excitement is a distraction from the horror of destruction and death."

Brenda retorts. "I don't care about death. Living is shit."

Sandra's eyes are fixed on Brenda. "You're right, living is shit. But it's not meant to be. There is a place better than this and we only get there by killing the way we think, then giving birth to a new way of thinking."

Brenda is silent for a moment, then she says, "Thinking different can't help me."

Sandra's eyes are dead serious. "It can," she replies.

"It can't yeah, it can't!" shouts Brenda. Sandra chases after her until Brenda stops in the middle of the road.

"You can't help me, yeah. Nuffing didn't help me yeah. When my mum stabbed me, yeah. Nuffing can't help." Brenda breaks down and cries. She wants change. She wants happiness without the grime. Most of all she needs genuine love that will comfort and shield her from the destruction. Sandra pulls Brenda close and hugs her tightly.

After the tears have dried, Sandra calls her office and reports the situation and someone goes to investigate. That someone is Ms McNeal. In the meantime, Sandra takes Brenda out for something to eat.

Chapter Sixty-Five

THE STEAK HOUSE is expensive-looking. Sandra and Brenda sit opposite each other in the cushioned, red leather booth.

Salad and a large piece of grilled steak fills Sandra's plate. Brenda has a burger and chips with a large coke.

Sandra sips on her mineral water then speaks. "You find school boring, don't you?"

"Yeah, school's shit innit? The teachers don't like me."

"And why don't they like you ?"

"I don't know. They say I got learning difficulties and I'm disruptive to other pupils."

Brenda is staring at her plate, playing with the food. Sandra takes a few more bites of steak, watching Brenda closely before replying.

"You know what? You ain't got learning difficulties, they've got teaching difficulties." Sandra's words feel like a big warm hug. Brenda looks up with half a smile. Sandra continues.

"I'm gonna tell you something and you should never forget it. There is real magic deep within your soul and that makes you as an individual the highest value in the universe and gives you the power to understand anything innit. I mean anything, you listening? So when they say you will never be able to understand something, you tell them it's only time which separates you from knowing that something."

Brenda is quiet. She doesn't know how to respond. What is this woman telling her, that she is a God? That she is bigger than God and all the other higher authorities around her? Or is Sandra planting seeds to help an innocent mind see through the dishonesty, force and fraud that this world builds upon and which spreads ignorance and kills billions.

Sandra's phone rings. "4125. Yes, speaking. Unh-unh, unh-unh, yes, I understand." Sandra clicks off the phone.

With sad eyes she looks at Brenda. "I'm so sorry, the senior social worker has recommended you go back home."

Brenda has a lump in her throat – it's full of disappointment. "But why?" she asks.

Sandra hesitates before she replies. "She feels the situation with the stabbing was a one-off and won't be repeated as long as your mother gets the help she needs."

"But I can't go home, I don't want to go home."

Sandra holds Brenda's hand. "Don't worry, I'll do my best to get this decision changed, just hold tight for a while and I will get you out of there."

Brenda pulls her hand away. "How long do I have to wait?

"A couple of days at the most," replies Sandra. "Come on, let's go."

Chapter Sixty-Six

THE RADIO IS PLAYING soothing music. Sandra is doing seventy down the connecting dual carriageway to Brenda's town. Brenda didn't finish her food at the steak house. She picked around the burger, ate all the bread and left the meat and a few chips. She drank the glass of coke plus two more.

She is twisting in the seat holding her belly. Her thoughts travel deep and wide regarding what Sandra said earlier.

Am I really the highest value in the universe? If so, why do I feel like the lowest, and can I really understand anything in the universe? How much time will that really take? We can't live forever, or maybe we can. If we can understand anything, that must mean we can understand death and stop it. Would that make us the highest value in the universe?

Brenda's thoughts stop. She frowns, then looks out of the window. For some reason she feels Sandra won't be coming back for her and she will have no choice but to go back to the grime, where she'll live out the remainder of her life with doses of short-term happiness mixed with harsh consequences until her soul rots away and she eventually dies.

As Sandra pulls off the dual carriageway, the pain in Brenda's belly increases. She squeezes down on it and clenches her teeth as the car drives past the signposts to her borough.

Chapter Sixty-Seven

BRENDA SITS IN HER room, smoking. Sandra had dropped her off three hours ago. Fasard put on a good act – the house was clean, she was clean, and her eyes were bright. She had a big smile for the reunion with her daughter. Brenda didn't know what to make of it, so she went to her room and waited for something to jump off.

Her phone rings. She leaps towards her jean jacket and pulls out the phone. "Hello?"

It's Sandra. She tells Brenda that she got the decision changed and is coming to pick her up in a few hours. Brenda can't believe it and jumps around the room with excitement.

Five hours have passed and Sandra hasn't arrived. Brenda is lying on the bed, face down. She had got tired of staring out the window four hours ago. Her phone rings and she quickly answers.

"Yeah, hello, I'm coming." She pauses on hearing a man's voice on the line. It's Shun. He's outside her block. "What's up, Bee?"

"Um. Um, who's dis?" she stammers.

"How mean, who's dis? It's me, innit?"

"Err, where are you, babes?"

Shun grips the steering wheel and looks up towards Brenda's block. "I'm outside, come downstairs."

Brenda stalls. "Um, how did you get out, babes?" She steps towards the window.

"Don't watch dat, just come downstairs, man."

Brenda swallows hard. "But, um, I can't."

Shun's voice rises. "What? Ah, don't fuck me you know? Come downstairs, man."

Brenda pleads, "But the social worker, she's coming for me soon. I have to go with her."

Shun lowers his voice. "Oi, Bee, don't you love me? Oi, you think them people business 'bout you? Nah, they don't. They can't do nuffing for you. Me and you are gonna be together forever, no matter what."

"Yeah, but."

Shun cuts in. "No buts. Don't get me mad. What, are you gonna choose the boy-dem over me? I'm not gonna ask you again. Come downstairs."

Brenda almost chokes and cries. She looks out of the window hoping Sandra will at that very moment come round the corner and save her.

"Oi, Bee, are you there?"

Brenda finds her voice. She knows Sandra won't be coming to save her. "Yeah," she begins reluctantly, "alright, babes, I'll be down in a minute."

Brenda ends the call and her heart feels heavy and sad as she makes her way back to the grime. She grabs up her jean jacket and steps out the door and down the stairs. Fasard doesn't notice or hear Brenda leaving as she sits in the kitchen with her alcohol and a box of twenty cigarettes. Brenda opens the front door and runs down the concrete stairs towards Shun's car.

Chapter Sixty-Eight

WEED SMOKE FILLS the car. Brenda almost chokes as she steps in. Shun gets off the phone and turns down the music. He leans over and sucks on Brenda's lips, then moves back in his chair. He takes a big pull on his spliff.

"So what happen at station?"

"Nuffing innit. They let me go."

"Yeah, but what did you tell them."

"Nuffing. When they found out my real age and name they stopped the interview, innit? Then a solicitor came and he told me to say 'no comment', so I did. Then they let me go and said I might be called back."

Shun begins to smile. He knows he has a soldier. He remembers times with certain other dudes being under a bit of the boy-dem pressure. They would start spitting, revealing the whole move, full names and address.

"Yeah, you dun good, shorty, you dun good. Eya bun dis."

Shun gives Brenda the spliff. Before she pulls on it, Brenda says with excitement in her voice. "Yeah, like how did you get out, doh?"

With serious eyes, Shun answers. "The reason why this game is so sweet is because the people we stick up are criminals themselves. What are they gonna say we took from them? Half a key in work, thirty gees in drugs money? Nah. You can even murder them and buss case, standard."

"How?" asks Brenda.

"Because the boy-dem need confessions or statements from the victims and I dun told you they're all criminals."

Brenda looks worried; she knows about street justice. "But what about if their peoples come back for revenge."

"Don't worry 'bout dat. They're fake ones like most others – they're scared of dying. They don't want to die right now. They're not like me and my crew. We don't mind dying today or tomorrow. When we got our sticks, we empty our clips. You listenin'? No long ting." Shun finishes rolling another spliff and licks it wet. He lights it and blows out smoke. He knows his words of streetsphilos would, like the weed smoke, subtly poison Brenda's young mind.

Shun starts the car and changes the subject.

"Oi, Bee, don't worry 'bout the social worker dem. You're with me now – my wifey till the end."

Brenda smiles. She spins around, her eyes hoping till the last moment that Sandra will appear. The car jerks forward. Brenda swallows some spit and closes her eyes then snuggles her body into the chair, heading back to the grime, as Shun drives off.

Chapter Sixty-Nine

THREE MONTHS HAVE passed since Brenda left
with Shun. Within that time, he had caused mayhem
on the streets, bringing Brenda along for the ride.

Today's a cold December day and Shun's been on
the block since morning, up to no good. Brenda stands
in front of the mirror rubbing her belly. She presses
down on it. She feels it kick. The bedroom door swings
open and Brenda pulls down her jumper and turns
towards Shun. He has a wide smile on his face.

"Come, Bee, I've got a move for us."

Brenda sits down on the bed. She's scared of being
brought on any more moves where Shun would stick-
up the young stick-up kids and rob shotters for their
money. She moans, "Oh, I don't feel well."

The atmosphere in the room turns sour. Shun screws
up his face and bops over to the bed.

"How mean you don't feel well? You ain't felt well
for the past two weeks. Nah, man, I need you now.
Don't get me mad. I need you on this move now!"

Brenda runs her hand over her belly.

"But, like. I think I'm pregnant." Tears are nearly in her eyes. Shun's eyes soften for a minute then turn hard again.

"Stop chatting shit. You think I care if you're pregnant? Get up, man." Shun slaps and kicks Brenda off the bed and towards the door. Brenda shouts and holds her belly. She knows it's no use trying to fight. Shun would just end up knocking her out.

Chapter Seventy

SHUN HAD BEEN watching his prey for a couple of weeks. He wasn't sure what this well-dressed, flossing guy does for a living, but he guessed it must be something against the law.

The guy in question had grown up in the same borough as Shun, but had recently moved into the block near Shun's house. He worked from home, running a multi-million pound publishing business through the Internet, employing thousands of mini-entrepreneurial workers around the globe.

Every mid-afternoon the man would pull up in his ride in a tracksuit. Some days he would have the same black bag, other days he wouldn't. Shun is convinced the bag has either money or drugs in it, and today he's gonna peel it.

He tells Brenda to wait in the car near the estate block and get ready to drive. Shun is charged as he explains the rest of the move. He seems filled with what drives a businessman – the challenge of building a new business and creating new value and jobs for others. But unlike the businessman, Shun's child-like, bigger than life adventure is short-term.

The man in his cold, heavy car, passes Brenda and Shun and drives towards the entrance of his block. Shun pulls down his cap over his eyes and checks for Betty Sue stuck in his waist.

"I'll be back in a minute." He jumps out of the car.

Chapter Seventy-One

SHUN JOGS SLOWLY towards the flossed-out car. The man has just finished parking and seems unaware of the approaching danger.

Shun slows down. He is two cars away. He places his palm over the handle of the gun and smiles as he sees the man reach for the bag on the back seat.

With no more time to think, Shun goes for the door handle. To his surprise, the door pops open. He doesn't see it but he hears it and feels it. The man pops off two shots into Shun's belly. Shun goes down holding his pistol, the man closes his car door and drives off as if nothing happened.

It takes about thirty seconds for Brenda's reaction. It seems like she is watching a movie. She jumps out of the car with a silent scream and runs towards Shun.

Blood is everywhere. She cries for Shun not to die. Shun holds his body still and makes no sound. He tries to firm it like a gee, but it's no use. He coughs blood and as the heat from the bullet storms through his body, he slowly says to Brenda, "Oi...Bee...get rid of the strap," and slowly, tears roll down his cheek.

Brenda grabs the gun from him, quickly gets herself together and breezes to the other end of the block towards the dustbin chutes.

Before she can make her way back to her bleeding cousin, blue sirens are on the way. Brenda makes a detour and ducks away from the scene. She ends up at Shun's house.

The man in his flossed-out car drives smoothly past the on-coming blue flashing lights. Of course he knows he can never go back to his home, but that doesn't bother him too much, for his business can be operated from anywhere in the world. What really bothers the man is the destruction he has left behind. He had seen Shun approaching him in the rear-view mirror and sensed something was going to jump off from his own days, when he had committed robberies as a poverty-driven child. The only thing was that in those days it was fists, not guns. The tools had changed but the techniques were the same.

The man pulls over in an alleyway. He takes off the tracksuit that he had run three miles in earlier. He opens his bag, pulls out his business suit with matching tie and shoes, slips them on, then smoothly starts the engine and drives off.

Chapter Seventy-Two

BRENDA HAS BEEN vomiting on and off for the past couple of hours. She holds on to the chrome toilet flusher and spits out the last of the fluids. She coughs and stands up, holding her belly. She looks at the four corners of the cell. A tear comes to her eye as she sits down on the wooden bed and holds her head.

It was about two weeks later that the police had finally caught up with her. Brenda wonders who informed– it must have been one of those Neighbourhood Watch people. The police had kicked off her Auntie Caprishus' door, which made Caprishus cuss Brenda out. She shouted through the door as the police were putting Brenda into the van, "A dutty gal, don't put your foot back into my yard again."

Brenda hears the noise of the latch slamming open. She needs to get her head straight to get out of this one. She plans on saying no comment, because she knows the boy-dem have no proof of her involvement.

But, as usual, the police are going to try their luck. At the end of the day, a man is in intensive care, they have found a potential murder weapon and they have a sighting of a third person on the scene.

A slim policewoman steps into the cell and tells Brenda they're ready for her. Brenda moves slowly from the bed and out the cell door.

Chapter Seventy-Three

"ARE YOU READY YET?"

The police officer behind the counter looks up from the desk with eyes that seem annoyed. He raises his crooked finger in the air and says, "One minute."

Sandra places her palms face down on the counter and waits. In a flash, noise fills the empty police waiting room. First, six people enter, some with complaints against others, some with things to produce. Next, three plainclothes officers appear behind the seated officer. As one of the plainclothes hands over a piece of paper, the door to Sandra's left opens. A tall greying male officer pops his head out. "Is a Miss Sandra Secret here?"

Sandra twists her head towards him. "Hi, that's me." She turns her body fully and extends her hand.

"Hi, I'm Sergeant King," replies the Sergeant.

As Sandra steps through the door, she sees Brenda sitting in a glass room behind a small grey desk.

Brenda cannot hear what Sandra and the officer are saying, but she knows for sure that she's going home.

Earlier, when she left the cell, they were telling her if she didn't start giving some answers, she may never get home. Brenda stood firm. She was scared but she made no comment; even when the government solicitor was advising her to talk, Brenda still refused. In the end, that is what saved her. Because they had nothing solid, they had to let her go.

Brenda watches as the conversation ends. The officer doesn't look pleased as he opens the door to set her free.

Brenda moves slowly from the desk and out of the glass room, then out of the police station. Sandra is close behind.

Chapter Seventy-Four

BRENDA AND SANDRA are standing in silence in the open air outside the police station. Sandra closes her eyes as she wonders whether to explain that at the last moment the decision to remove her from her mother was changed and she ended up in a meeting that lasted for five hours to find out why. She opens her eyes and looks at the expression on Brenda's face that says she doesn't care – she only cares about her disappointment at being let down. Brenda places her hand on her pregnant belly. Sandra finds the right words to break the ice: "How far along are you?"

Brenda is about to answer but is overcome by tears. "Why?" she asks as she covers her mouth.

"Why, why?" More tears flood Brenda's face. Sandra embraces her and holds her tightly as if Brenda were a newborn baby.

Brenda cries more tears on Sandra's shoulder until Sandra eases her off, holds her firmly and wipes away the tears. She speaks in a motherly voice. "I'm sorry. Its gonna be okay. You're safe now, you and your child."

Sandra embraces Brenda again and they stand there as the rain comes down.

Chapter Seventy-Five

FREEZING HAILSTONES are hitting the windshield as Sandra drives Brenda to a secure home where she'll have access to a new learning centre and a new life for her and her child, away from the grime.

The inside of the car is warm and comforting. Brenda feels like she could stay there forever, escaping the cold world. Her eyes close and she thinks about what her new life will be like – it makes her feel afraid but excited. The car stops

"Do you want something to eat?"

Her eyes open and she nods. As Sandra is getting out of the car, Brenda stops her. "Why is life this way?"

Sandra turns towards Brenda and takes her hand off the ignition. She takes a deep breath. "Do you remember when I mentioned being bored at school?"

Brenda nods.

"Well, boredom produces the need for excitement, which controls our every action."

"So why do they make school boring?"

Sandra thinks before she speaks. "To make money.

Think about it – if they have a billion people bored in their jobs and bored with learning their knowledge, they have a market to sell their destructive products to. That's why so many people are hooked on all sorts of drugs – from sugar to cocaine."

Brenda's eyes are open and alert; she wants to know more.

Sandra continues, "There is one way to get rid of the boredom and be free from destruction. That is to learn how to create new productive values for others. The word create is important; it means we have found harmony with the universe; we have found happiness."

Brenda stares off into space. She rubs her stomach, then asks, "Isn't the baby in here a creation?"

Sandra smiles. "Yes, Brenda, it sure is, and a beautiful one at that. And that little creation will bring you a world of happiness only if you have enough money to raise it. If not, it will bring you nothing but struggle, pain and unhappiness. Do you understand that?"

Brenda nods her head. Sandra pinches Brenda's chin as she says, "Wait here in the warmth. I'll be back in a moment." Sandra hurries towards the shop.

Chapter Seventy-Six

BRENDA SITS CONTENTLY with the warm air blowing and music playing low in the background. She's dreaming of the big house she'll live in with her daughter, both of them playing with the most beautiful dollhouse ever made. Before she can dream any more her phone rings. Brenda's heart skips a beat as she answers.

"Yeah, hello?"

It's Shun calling her from the hospital.

He asks her where she is and who she's with.

She tells him.

He tells her he's getting out of the hospital tomorrow and wants her to be at his house with the money he stashed at her mum's crib.

She tells him the situation with his mum, Caprishus.

He tells her to just be cool, his mum is a drunk and she don't remember nothing.

Brenda plucks up some courage and fights away the Love-Jones creeping through her bones. Firmly, she tells him no, and he can go and get the money for himself because she's going to go with Sandra. Then something happens she never expected. Shun starts crying, telling her he loves her and needs her and that he wants to get out of the grime. He says he has plans to use the money to go legit so that they can raise their baby together, away from the grime. Brenda rubs her belly and at that moment everything falls into place. She grins, as her dream now includes Shun, the love of her life, the big house, her child and that beautiful dollhouse.

Her focus moves from straight–ahead, across the dashboard towards the steering wheel. The car key is dangling in the air. Brenda's heart heaves as she contemplates stealing the car. She rubs her belly again and feels it kick. Brenda slides behind the steering wheel, tells Shun she loves him too, ends the call and puts the car into gear. She looks out of the window and sees Sandra coming towards her. Just before Brenda drives off, she says farewell as her eyes meet with Sandra's.

The car screeches away from the pavement, leaving Sandra's unsurprised reflection in the rear-view mirror.

Chapter Seventy-Seven

BRENDA IS SPEEDING DOWN the narrow streets, hoping to get the money from her house before the boy-dem get there. She is over-excited and plays her dream over and over again in her mind's eye until she can feel the happiness consume her and take her mind into another world.

After ten minutes of driving, Brenda pulls up at her house and runs up the concrete stairs, and into her bedroom.

On entering her room, things turn sour. She knows straight away that something is missing. She begins tipping her bedroom upside down. It dawns on her that the money is gone. She doesn't want to accept reality, so she turns the place over again.

Stressed but not confused, Brenda holds her belly and meets the floor with her knees. She knows it must have been her mother who took the money. And Brenda knows it's gone for good – her mother would have spunked it out in one day.

She also knows that going downstairs to fight her

mother would not bring it back. But it seems that her mother may have flopped her show and ruined her chance for happiness.

Brenda has to release her anger. She gets off the floor and goes to find her mother.

Chapter Seventy-Eight

BRENDA FINDS HER MOTHER the first place she looks – sitting at the kitchen table drunk, smoking on a long cigarette.

Fasard looks up from the ashtray and licks her dry lips, stubs out the half-finished cigarette and immediately lights another one.

"Oi, mum, where's my money?" Brenda's face is serious.

Fasard blows her smoke in Brenda's direction. "What money?"

"The money I had in my room, innit." Brenda's blood is boiling.

Fasard's eyes are closed. She raises her left palm in the air about shoulder high and says, "Laydee, laydee. I don't want to argue with you, lady, now go and sit down."

Brenda watches as her mother opens her eyes, picks up her drink, takes a long gulp then closes them again. She pulls on her cigarette and sits there as though she has never been disturbed from her liquored-up state.

Brenda sucks on her teeth and moves towards her mother. The moment she puts her hand down on her mother's blouse, Fasard reacts.

"What the rass you doing?!" Fasard's arms fly wildly up in the air, making her jump out of the chair.

"I want my money, innit? I want my money," demands Brenda as she rubs away the cigarette ash that burnt her arm.

Fasard moves away from her daughter and says, "Just stay away from me, yeah."

"Nah, I want the money that you took. Nah, I want my money. I don't care."

"I AIN'T GOT NO MONEY!" screams Fasard. "LOOK!" Fasard pops open her blouse and rips away her bra. "See? I ain't got no money. Now leave me alone!" Fasard grips her head and screams for help like a mad woman as the cigarette burns through the lino.

Brenda looks at her mother in disgust, picks up the cigarette and stubs it out, then turns and walks out of the kitchen leaving her mother on her knees to scream the house down.

Chapter Seventy-Nine

PRESSURE AND STRESS have never hit the thirteen-year-old like this before. So much has happened during the past few days that Brenda has forgotten it is Christmas Eve. She has been driving around in the night for a while until she ends up outside Shun's house.

She wonders if the boy-dem have been there already, looking for her. She hopes that they have. Just in case, she parks the car in the underground garages of the housing blocks.

Brenda walks back through the estate towards Shun's house.

Brenda knocks and one of her cousins answers. He doesn't stop to say much, he just leaves the door open and tells her, "Later."

She goes straight up to Shun's room without any bother and falls onto his bed. Brenda thinks for a while. *'What will I tell Shun? How will he react? It's no biggie – he did say he loves me. We just have to work out a new moneymaking plan together.'* Brenda's thoughts drift off into a beautiful dream.

When she wakes, she's in pain. She runs to the bathroom and curls into a ball on the floor. The pain disappears for a moment and Brenda holds the bathtub to ease herself up from the floor. Then, all of a sudden, her eyes open wide. She feels another sharp pain shoot down her spine. It's so furious it brings her to her knees. More pain takes the wind out of her and Brenda falls on her back as water covers the floor. Brenda shouts at the top of her lungs as another earth-shattering grip of pain overwhelms her.

"OH, GOD, HELP!"

As usual, "God" is silent. Brenda flips her body upright. She can feel something wedged outside her vagina. She slowly reaches down and makes contact with a hairy object.

She begins to say, "Oh, shit, what's that?" before common sense tells her she's giving birth. Her body flips back towards the floor and she screams in low grunts while catching air through her nose and letting it out of her mouth in fast repetition.

The oxygen in the small bathroom is running out fast. Brenda feels like she's about to die as the baby slips, almost by itself, out of her vagina and onto the bathroom floor.

Chapter Eighty

BRENDA LAYS PERFECTLY STILL, afraid to sit up and look at what is lying between her legs. Then, like a fire engine siren, it starts. Low at first, then rising higher and higher, flooding the bathroom with screams.

Brenda sits up slowly with her eyes still closed. The screaming and crying gets louder. Brenda opens her tear-filled eyes and looks. At first, she can't work out why it seems sort of weird, then she realises that it's lying flat on its face.

Automatically, Brenda picks up her baby and pulls it towards her with maternal love. The umbilical cord flies out of her womb unnoticed.

Brenda holds the baby away from her to take a better look. The long stringy piece of flesh attached to the baby's stomach almost makes Brenda drop the baby back on the floor. The umbilical cord scares her but the bright glowing eyes now fixed on her removes the fear and gives her strength. She gets up from the floor. The baby is no longer crying as she holds it to her shoulder and pulls down her T-shirt over her thighs. She looks for something to wrap the baby in but the only thing she can find is a jumper. Brenda slips the baby's legs into the neck of the jumper until its whole body is covered. Once again, the noise of the crying baby fills the room. Brenda cradles it to her chest and paces the bathroom saying, "Shhhh, okay, baby, shhhh," when a knock interrupts her.

Chapter Eighty-One

BRENDA STOPS PACING. The baby is still crying when there is another knock at the door.

"Um, yeah, who is it?" she says.

"How mean who is it? Open up the door."

'Shit,' Brenda says to herself. It's Auntie Caprishus.

Caprishus, who is now an anti-depressant addict who spends most of her time drunk up in her room, but whenever she leaves her room it would be for a good reason or a change of routine. When this happened, she would cause mayhem, swearing and cussing everyone from the 'Devil' to anyone that might be in her house.

Another knock. Brenda holds her breath. She knows it's all on top. Brenda slowly opens the door and the baby stops crying.

At first Caprishus doesn't speak. Maybe she's trying to remember who Brenda is.

"Wait, what you doing in here?"

Brenda doesn't answer.

"A girl child. What you doing in here? And whose

baby dat?" Caprishus' huge chest heaves up and down as she waits for a reply.

"It's mines, auntie, mines and Shun's baby." Now Brenda waits for a reply.

A weird expression comes across Caprishus' face. Brenda wonders if her auntie even remembers her or her son. She's got so many.

"Shun?" Caprishus begins, sounding confused. "Shun don't have no rass picknee. A dutty gal don't budder push nah picknee pun my son."

Caprishus is about to flipmode. "Come, tek your nasty self out of my house, yeah. You think Shun gonna want nasty bitch like you?"

Brenda doesn't move. She moans, "But, auntie."

"I SAID GET OUT OF MY HOUSE!" Yells Caprishus. A tear comes to Brenda's eye. The baby starts bawling. Brenda runs out of the bathroom and into Shun's room. She puts down the baby and begins putting on her clothes. She can still hear her auntie cussing.

"That's all you young girls are good for, walk and breed. That's why no man nah want you. And you can't get nah job. You nah have no education. You don't wanna go school. All you wanna do is walk road and look man. You is a bitch, that's why I don't keep women friend. You hear what I said? Me don't want you in yah. Come tell lie pun me son. It's due to you why him get shot. Me say me nah want you in yah. Come out of my house!"

Brenda steps out of the bedroom, holding her baby now covered in a multicoloured towel. She doesn't look at her auntie as she heads for the front door. Her auntie carries on talking.

"Yes, get out of my house, you nasty bitch. About she yah come call me auntie."

Chapter Eighty-Two

THE CHAPPING DECEMBER wind blows relentlessly across Brenda's face. Everything that isn't moving seems frozen to the floor. Brenda pulls the hood on her tracksuit top further down her face and picks up the pace towards Sandra's car. She wishes she hadn't parked it three roads over as the weight of the baby is making the walk a struggle.

On the second road, she stops at a phone box to call and tell Shun what happened. Before she can enter, she has to wait for a little old lady and her mongrel dog to leave. The old lady stares at Brenda as she steps out of the phone box. Brenda takes no notice as she steps inside, fumbles in the top pocket of her jean jacket and pulls out her phone. Brenda turns her head to see if the old bat is still looking back at her.

Brenda sucks on her teeth and presses quick dial for Shun's number.

Shun answers.

Brenda breaks down all that has happened.

Shun shouts and curses.

Brenda cries for forgiveness.

Shun curses and shouts some more.

Brenda asks Shun if he still loves her.

Shun says, "Yes, but you flop my show. It's a long ting to make back that, pees now."

Brenda replies that she loves him too and so does his baby she's holding in her arms. She says it won't take long to go on a couple of moves and stack for a while then use the pees to build a legal business. Then they can escape the grime and live happily ever after.

Shun goes quiet and the phone disconnects. Brenda calls back. The phone is answered quicker than normal and it's a female voice.

"Can I speak to Shun?"

"Who? Who's dis?" says the female voice.

"This is Brenda. Can I speak to Shun, please? The phone goes quiet... the female voice speaks. "Shun don't want to talk to you."

Brenda loses her voice.

"This is his woman speaking. Don't ever call back this phone again." The line goes dead.

A sinking feeling takes over Brenda's body. She feels dead inside. She doesn't know what to make of what just happened. Her first reaction is to call back. She breaks down and cries as the phone is switched off. A gust of wind whips at her exposed ankles, pushing her into movement. Brenda exits the box and heads for the car in tears and with a pain that's as deep as a knife cut.

Chapter Eighty-Three

BRENDA DRIVES THE CAR through the empty, cold Christmas streets until the petrol runs out. The baby is asleep as Brenda exits the car and begins walking. She can't think straight, but she needs a new plan. She wishes someone could think for her and make everything all right and make the pain vanish. She turns a corner and begins to walk up a rich middle-class road as other thoughts flood her mind. She hears the cussing from her auntie and the words from that woman's mouth on the other end of Shun's phone. She remembers the one word her mother used to start almost every sentence: NO. "NO, I ain't got no money", "NO, I can't take you there", "NO, there's none left." Then finally she remembers what Sandra had said about the difference between raising a child when you're poor and raising one when you're rich.

Brenda closes her eyes. A plan flashes before her. Somehow she'll get rich and come back for her child, buy that big house and that beautiful dollhouse and live out her dream of happiness. Brenda opens her eyes and looks down at her child, sleeping so still and heavenly. She whispers in the child's ear, "Mummy is gonna get you used to living in a big house until she come for you."

Brenda kisses her child and stops outside the house with the biggest driveway. It looks so welcoming and warm – she knows this is the place for her child.

Brenda makes the right choice because the people who live in this house are super value creators. Sandra had talked about becoming one of these people – the real heroes of the world, who society will rely on to provide productive goods and stimulating jobs. At present, without them and people like them, there would be no social security, no homes, no food, no nothing. And nowhere for Brenda to drop her responsibility.

Brenda steps onto the driveway. In the same instant the front door opens to reveal a departing guest. Brenda quickly ducks back out the gate and around the wall. She clutches the baby tightly to her chest and listens to the people talking. Brenda has to think quickly: carry on walking with the baby or leave it somewhere else? But where?

Brenda hears the sound of feet walking on the pebbled driveway. Her eyes dart around wildly, looking for somewhere to leave her child. Opposite the house is an overflowing yellow skip. Brenda runs across the road. The only suitable thing to put her child on is a soiled mattress. Brenda puts her baby down and, without looking back, breaks into a sprint up the street. Before Brenda reaches the corner, the screams of her abandoned child enter the depths of her very being. Automatically, she feels the need to stop and go back, but her legs seem to have a life of their own. She keeps on running like a thief in the night.

Images of her baby are now flashing through Brenda's mind at a hundred miles a minute. This produces instant guilt and tears. Brenda cries until her eyes were almost popping out of their sockets.

Back at the skip, it's no different for her child, who cries in the same way in the trash heap.

Chapter Eighty-Four

THAT CHRISTMAS DAY left two kids abandoned. Both are innocent – or are they? Did they deserve what their situation gave them? Can God really help them break out of their trap? Is religion the answer or does it only deliver a temporary escape from the trap? In the end, will it sink one further into the trap until one is dead?

But Brenda no longer cares. All that matters is finding a way to get rich quick without the harsh consequences of the grime. Unfortunately, her knowledge is limited, so she stands there in an off-licence surrounded by wall-to-wall beverages, hoping to get the answer from Mr Alcohol.

She digs into her pocket and looks at her last few coins – not enough to buy sweets and a drink.

She looks up at the shop owner and notices he hasn't taken his eyes off his paper – not even when she first entered and made the shop bell ring. She feels that he must be another shop worker who hates his job and has lost interest in stopping shoplifters.

Brenda spins around to the fridge cooler and removes a can of beer. She swiftly puts it in her pocket and calmly moves towards the door. She pulls on the handle, but the door doesn't budge.

"Please, young lady, put back the drink," says Pepi, the shop owner, calmly. He is a hardworking business-man with a receding hairline and old eyes with huge dark circles around them. Probably from working in his business night and day seven days a week without paying attention to seasonal holidays.

Brenda turns a different colour.

"I ain't got no drink. Just open the door, man. I ain't took no drink." Brenda lies desperately, but it's no good because when she thought Pepi was reading his paper, he was actually watching her on his video mon-itor below his till counter.

Chapter Eighty-Five

"**NOW DON'T BE SILLY**. I saw you take the drink. Put back the drink."

Brenda gets mad and begins shaking the door and shouting, "Listen, yeah, I ain't got no drink, yeah. Just let me out of the shop, what's wrong with you. Let me out the shop!"

Pepi squeals incoherently with fury and runs out from behind his counter. In his haste he accidentally switches off the security lock. The door clicks open.

Brenda doesn't expect it and slams the door back shut before she can pull the door open again. Pepi is behind her and pulling at her jacket.

"You thieving little bitch. Give me back what you stole."

"Leave me alone," screams Brenda, frantically trying to struggle free from Pepi's grip. The shop bell rings. It goes unnoticed by Pepi and Brenda.

The customer watches for a while then intervenes.

"Oi, what's the problem here?"

Pepi stops pulling and turns towards the voice. The

man is much larger than his voice sounds, but this doesn't faze Pepi, for he's a fearless man when it comes to defending his business. He responds without thinking, "This is none of your bloody business. So just piss-off, ah." Pepi knows he made a mistake his left eye twitches. He releases Brenda and prepares for one to the chin.

The man expands his chest and laughs to himself. "Oi, you listenin'? I've learnt never to make a bad situation worse, so I'm gonna tell you what I'm gonna do for you tonight. I'm gonna let you tell me what this girl has done to upset you. Then I'm gonna fix the problem."

Pepi swallows nervously, calms his heart rate down, then speaks. "She took a drink from my fridge without paying."

Brenda cuts in, "Don't lie, I never take no drink."

The man turns to Brenda and waves her down, turning back to Pepi. "Will this cover the drink?" He pulls out some notes and hands one over. Pepi takes it. The man pulls Brenda to his side and leads her to the door.

"Wait," Pepi begins to say. "You have change." But the shop door has already closed.

Chapter Eighty-Six

THE AIR FEELS DIFFERENT as Brenda walks down the road with this stranger who saved her from her predicament. Or is he a stranger? His face definitely seems familiar.

"Brenda, you don't remember me, do you?"

Brenda is thinking hard; she shakes her head from side to side and says, "Nooo, I don't think so."

"Well, I remember you."

"Where from?" Brenda quizzes him.

"Oi, that's not important. What is important, I got something to offer you."

For a brief moment there is silence, then it finally clicks. Brenda knows who the stranger is. She had gone to school with him where he was three years above her. Back then people called him Sav, but his full name is Savant. She remembered him looking like a neek and a bit of a brain box, but now he has transformed into a cold smooth top-boy.

"What I got to offer?" Savant stops himself to think. "Nah, let me tell you what someone once told me. To solve problems you have to be honest." Savant looks at Brenda to see if he has her attention before continuing. "So that must mean the cause of problems is dishonesty. What's one of the biggest problems they talk about on TV? I'll tell you; drugs-cocaine and heroin. But why that's so sick is that the boy-dem only have to use honesty. Make all drugs legal, ending the drug underworld, and boom– all problems solved. But they don't, because they profit from being dishonest. So they rely on the poverty-driven people they created to get into drugs. The more of us that get involved means more jobs for them. Without us they have no jobs, you over?"

They both stop next to a heavy ride. Savant leans on it as Brenda leans on the wall opposite. He continues talking. "As long as the shotter don't let them" – Savant points at a window that has a neighbourhood watch sticker on it – "or any other informer like them, see his hustle, the boy-dem will pretend they ain't seen nothing and leave the shotter alone." Savant pulls out his car key, grins, then adds, "But what's still all sweeter than that is a female shotter, specially one with big tits and hips." Brenda shows her teeth and blushes.

Savant continues, "Now, believe me, my shit is tight – no one will ever suspect that you're even shotting. Not the boy-dem or the mans-dem on the block, you feel me?"

Brenda smiles and nods her head. It's like Savant is an angel who has come to grant her wish. '*Maybe there is someone up there looking out for me,*' Brenda thinks. They both jump in the car and head towards making Brenda's dream a reality.

ACT THREE

Chapter Eighty-Seven

THE NEXT EIGHT MONTHS Brenda breaks it down like she never knew she could. She has money stacked in plastic bags and money stuffed in coat pockets. Her dream isn't far off; in fact, it's just around the corner. Brenda thinks she will have enough money in the next four months to retire from shotting for good and build a good life for her and her child. At the moment, she lives at the drug base in the heart of the ghetto where police or government officials never come. It's the perfect set-up – the outside resembles a normal mashed down ghetto house, but once you step inside you see evidence of a multi-million pound business.

Savant had recently bought the two houses next door so he could house his little army of female shotters, all dressed in slimline suits dropping off keys. His operation is tight and Brenda is a part of it. She smiles into her funky-shaped mirror and adjusts the thick, expensive, stylish belt.

"You sexy bitch," says a voice from behind.

Brenda turns around and breaks into another smile.

"Hi, babes," she begins, "what's up? What you saying?"

"Nuffing much," replies Pristine. Tall and slim with good skin, she's new to the game – only a month in – Brenda had shown her the ropes.

Pristine hands over Brenda's phone. "Ah, you left it on the table. You've got a message."

The message is from Savant, the text shows the details for Brenda's first client of the day. Brenda turns on her heels and picks up her ostrich-skin bag. "Ah, it's work," she says, flinging her bag over her shoulder.

"I'll be back soon yeah, babes. See you later."

"Yeah, later," says Pristine.

Chapter Eighty-Eight

THE MORNING SUN is hotter than usual. As it hits Brenda's face, it makes her feel good. She slides her sunglasses down onto her nose and hits the concrete streets. Just up ahead, she sees two of the usual mandem standing on the block. From the start of summer, Brenda had noticed them. They had been watching her closely. They even called out to her a few times, but she had blanked them and kept walking on the opposite side of the road.

This morning, she thinks she'll give one of them a chance. She gets herself ready to swish her hips extra hard as she crosses the road. The closer she gets the more worried she feels. Their faces are unsmiling. Brenda grips her bag tight and her hips stop swishing. She is three feet away from them when their expressions change. Brenda's full beauty hits them – she is stunning. Whatever they were thinking vanishes. Brenda senses it and quickly puts the swish back into her hips. She shines her sexy glare as she passes them.

Brenda has learnt how to handle boys. She puts a bit

more wiggle into her curvy backside, expecting the usual thing to happen. When it doesn't, Brenda casually turns her head to see what's up. It doesn't make any sense; not one of them has moved. They seem to be having an argument. So Brenda flicks back her head with attitude and walks away sexily.

Chapter Eighty-Nine

THE ARGUMENT CONTINUES between the mans-dem. "Hey, gee, you listening? She's heavy, blud. Rah she's fit." says one of the mans-dem to the other.

"Oi, forget bout dat. She needs to get peel, blud 'cause a snake told me that all them chicks we see in business suits, are not on a nine to five, u know? But they're shotting for that fassyhole, Savant."

"Yeah, but evendoh, she's a girl, doh, blud."

The other laughs at the last statement.

"Oi, cuzzy, don't be a dickhead. Hold on, you think people like the government has got time to think about oh, that person is a girl so we won't tax her? Nah, they're taxing everyone, blud, you feel me? And I'm like the government – I wanna peel everyone. So next time we see her she needs to get a bang-bang peel dem."

"We can't do that, doh, if she's shotting for Savant."

"So what? Don't be 'fraid of dem fools you know. He's a dickhead, he's a pussyhole. Dem boy der can't do man nuffing, you over?"

The running feet of Queenie, a short girl with narrow hips, a button nose, beady eyes, and thin lips interrupt the argument. She was once a worker for Savant who got high on his supply, lost her job, then turned to prostitution.

"Oi, you, jezzy, come here," one of them shouts. She ignores them and keeps on running through the housing blocks until she gets to the drug base.

Chapter Ninety

QUEENIE'S HAND IS trembling as she knocks on the door. She just clipped a wallet with over two hundred notes in it from a squeak she was giving head to. Queenie can't remember when she last had so much money to buy drugs with and she plans to cop and blow the whole lot.

The door opens halfway.

"Yeah, can I help you?" says Pristine.

Queenie licks her lips and hops from one foot to the other. "Yeah, yeah, is um… Sav der."

"Um, what do want with him?"

Queenie scratches her face and her eyes become alert. She realises that Pristine doesn't know her and that Savant is definitely in. Queenie begins to run game.

"Yeah, yeah um, I was sent to pick up some work." Queenie shows the bundle of notes and spins around nervously. "Yeah, you get me? He knows I'm coming."

Pristine hesitates. Queenie steps one foot in and Pristine opens the door wide. Savant appears at the end of the corridor.

"Oi, what's she doing in here?"

Pristine begins to speak but Queenie talks over her.

"Nah, listen, Sav, I've got money." She walks up towards Savant. "Just shot me whatever this can buy."

"Get out. I don't want nutting from you. Get out."

"Ah, come on. Please, man, please, man, just cop me su'um, please." begs Queenie, peering into the room behind Savant.

"You listening? Are you stupid? I don't do deals with junkies. Are you stupid?"

Queenie is in her own world – she isn't even hearing what Savant is saying.

"Ah, come on Sav, man, look how much works you got on the table. Shot me su'um, please!"

It's like a red light comes on in Savant's head and his eyes turn cold. He grabs Queenie by her throat and drags her kicking and choking towards the front door.

"Hey, listen, don't bring yourself to my door again, or I swear down you die this week." Savant kicks Queenie onto the street.

Chapter Ninety-One

OUTSIDE QUEENIE FLINGS her arms wildly in the air as she curses Savant out. She doesn't stop until she gets near the mans-dem. She gets an idea and crosses over to the mans-dem.

"Oi, Demi, Demi!" shouts Queenie a bit too loud.

"Oi, what rass you bawling out my name for? What's wrong with you," responds Demi, a large man with a neck that looks too narrow for his body.

"Nah, nah, I just want to tell you something."

"What?!, what?!, what?!" Demi moves towards Queenie.

Queenie feels she might be making a mistake but continues. "Nah, listen, I got some money here, but Sav won't shot me no work. So I was wondering if you could cop it for me."

Demi screws up his face. "Show me the papers."

Queenie pulls the money out of her bra. She knows from the look in Demi's eyes she has made a big mistake, but she is desperate.

She quickly tries to change Demi's thoughts. "And

the cunt's got piles of work in the yard you know, and he wouldn't sell me none."

Greed flashes across Demi's face. "Eya, give me the money den." Queenie hesitates. Demi quickly snatches the money.

"Oi!" shouts Queenie as she tries to grab her money back.

"Shut your mouth, you jezz," says Demi and gives her one to the face. She crumples to the ground.

He walks back over to Sweart, who is dressed in dark clothing. Sweart pleads, "What, give man a cut den?"

"Just cool, man, just cool," says Demi as he counts out the papers. "You're not ready for this, you're a shook one.

"How?" demands Sweart.

"Because you're shook, innit, you're boomee," retorts Demi. "You wanna be on the block like you're a badboy. What you think you're gonna come round, badboy, and not be a badboy? You listenin'? You gonna be a badboy today."

Sweart's heart jumps a beat, but he stays calm.

"You know what? We're gonna peel that pussy-hole," begins Demi. "He's in the yard now, blud, wid ber work."

"Yeah, how you know dat?"

"That cat told me, innit." Demi points at Queenie as she pulls herself off the ground.

"So what, you down den, yeah?" Demi doesn't wait for an answer. "Alright, I'm gonna go for my gat."

"Hold on, hold on, cuz," stammers Sweart. "There's

ber chicks in the yard ya-nah."

Demi stops. "What did I tell you from before, rude-boy? We're living in corruption, rudeboy. I will blaze chicks, mums and dads, standard. I'm a wicked man, you listening?"

Sweart butts in with fear in his voice. "But doing that will make man dead quick, rudeboy."

"Don't get it twisted. You wanna be a badboy you're gonna dead quick. It's not a game, it's real, you feel me? Like when you're going on a move you have to think like ter, you wanna die today? You wanna die now? Thinking like that makes man potent. You know bout them word potent? Means powerful, blud.

And them fake ones will know it. When they see man from afar they turn and walk the other way; they don't wanna buck up on the realness. Their fake is scared of the real, you feel me?"

On the surface Sweart looks scared, but Demi's twisted logic has given him a new dimension on how the badboy spirit operates.

"Oi, cuz." Demi's voice snaps Sweart out of his trance. "I'm coming back wid two sticks den, innit? And if we need to lick down chicks we lick down chicks. Standard, it's nuffing."

Sweart doesn't answer. Demi turns and jogs towards the housing blocks.

Chapter Ninety-Two

FROM THE MOMENT SAVANT kicked Queenie out he knew he had to move fast. He boxed up the last of the work and sent the boxes to his pick-up premises on motorcycle. He didn't wile up Pristine too much but told her if she made a mistake like that again, he would fire her. Then he told her to call him a cab for eleven o'clock.

At five to eleven the doorbell rings. Pristine goes to answer it. She is just about to say, 'You're a bit early,' when a big gun gets stuck in her face. Demi growls. "Shut your mouth, and you won't get hurt."

Demi and Sweart bundle inside the house, donning balaclavas. He dashes Pristine towards the door at the end of the corridor, her long slender arms flying in front of her like a puppet, her large breasts heaving up and down with a life of their own.

He shoves her through the door. Savant is sitting behind the table looking placid.

He talks slowly. "I know what you came for, but it's gone."

Demi cuts in, "Shut your mouth. How you know what we come for? Oi, hold this bitch." Demi throws Pristine to Sweart and walks up to Savant. He pulls off his balaclava, sticks his gun into Savant's chest and says, "Now that I've shown you my face, I'm gonna kill you."

Pristine screams; Savant stammers. "But, but, but, I told you what you want is gone, you can search the house. What's wrong with you?!" Savant is mad. He gets up in his rage. Demi licks Savant's nose bridge with the gun.

"Shut up!" shouts Demi. Savant curls up on the chair.

"You're gonna die today," Demi laughs insanely. "Don't worry, we all have to die someday." Demi steps back and aims the gun. Savant doesn't flinch. Pristine screams. "NO!" Sweart holds her tighter.

Before Demi opens his gun on Savant's face, he says with a twisted smile, "Bang-bang, peel dem."

Blood and bones decorate the wall. Pristine cries out and pulls away from Sweart's grip and runs for it. She doesn't get far as Demi unloads the rest of his clip into her back.

For the next fifteen minutes the pair ransack the house leaving nothing but death and destruction behind.

Chapter Ninety-Three

FIVE HOURS LATER, the mans-dem see Brenda from afar as they stand on the sixth floor landing of the housing block. She looks in a hurry.

"Oi, there's that chick," says Demi, pointing. His eyes are like an eagle.

"Where? Where?" Sweart stretches his body over the balcony.

"Up there, coming down the road. You know we're peeling her now doh, innit?" Demi waits for any objections. "Yeah, we're peeling her now, star, cause we didn't even get nutting from the yard."

Sweart moans, "Ah cuz, man, don't you think its bait? There's ber five-o, ber feds down there on the block."

Demi laughs. "Fuck the police. We're peeling her now, blud. I swear, don't get me mad. I'm gonna go for my stick. You go downstairs and stop her."

Sweart looks back over the balcony. Brenda is just a few yards away. He sucks on his teeth then turns and walks towards the stairs.

Demi shouts. "Make sure you stop her, ya-nah."
Sweart feels like replying, but just keeps on walking.

Chapter Ninety-Four

"PSST... **OI, BABES."**

This gets Brenda's attention. She stops in front of the housing block bin cupboard in a sexy stance. She has been holding thousands of Savant's money for the past three hours at the money drop spot. She has also rung his phone over twenty times without an answer. Worried, she is now hurrying back to the base to find out what's up. She plans on telling Sweart, who's walking towards her slowly, that she can't stop for long when a crusty hand with grime underneath its nails pulls her from behind and drags her into the bin cupboard.

At first, Brenda thinks she's going to be raped, until Demi speaks.

"Yeah, you know what it's about? Where's the pees?"

Immediately Brenda clutches her bag tight and regains her strength. She begins struggling and kicking. Her heel digs deep into Demi's left shin. He screams like a woman and throws Brenda against a metal bin.

"You little jeez," he growls, and lays down bone-shattering blow after blow. They ricochet throughout Brenda's body and brain, the pain is so intense she's pleading for her heart to stop beating.

Sweart enters. "Oi, bruv, you're gonna kill her!" His shout snaps Demi out of his craze. He stops pounding on Brenda and grips the bloody gun tight in his palm. He picks up her bag and spits. The last words Brenda hear from her attacker are, "This idiot jezz try go on like she's ruff."

Her grip loosens and the support from the large metal bin seems to disappear as she slides down towards the ground.

Chapter Ninety-Five

BLOOD DRIPS DOWN into the corner of Brenda's mouth. The taste of it shakes her out of unconsciousness. She grips her hands together but can't feel the bag. Her heart sinks and she doesn't want to move. She sits in the stinky bin-room for a while and cries bloodstained tears, until she is all cried out. Then she slowly, agonisingly rises from the ground and stumbles out.

Outside it's hotter than before the attack. The humid heat stings through the cut near her eye like a thousand needles.

Lethargically, Brenda begins to walk back to the drug base, holding her rib cage and drinking her blood from the wound on her lip. Every step is painful, so she pauses for a rest on a low wall. No one stops to offer help. She carries on until she's on the opposite side of the road from the base.

She doesn't understand it. The base seems to have disappeared. A short while passes before Brenda realises it's right in front of her – it's a taped off murder scene.

Her head sinks to the ground. She moves along the wall behind her, falls into the gap and onto the staircase. She sits there without a thought in her mind.

Chapter Ninety-Six

THE SURROUNDINGS SMELL of stale cake and cheesy feet, and Brenda is smothered in it as she lies stretched out on a sofa bed in what looks like a dining room. She has no clue how she got there or how long she's been there. The pain in her head is gone, but her left side still hurts when she breathes deeply.

She lifts her head up and looks towards the open door. Someone she doesn't recognise flashes past and she hears a voice.

"I see you're feeling better. Well, at least you're awake."

Brenda doesn't answer. She watches as Obese, 'the fat, blue-eyed devil,' uses all his energy to walk over and sit down in the frowzy chair opposite her.

"You know, I had to get two of my boys to bring you in here. You were hurt real bad. The streets are harsh."

Obese pulls his food trolley towards him and begins munching down on the stale assortment of food.

"You'd mud be 'ungry." As Obese speaks, food drops out of his mouth onto his large man-breast.

"You haven't eaten for almost two days." He gulps and swallows, then eats some more.

"You want something to eat?"

Brenda doesn't answer.

Obese shouts, "Tas, oi Tas, come here a second."

Tassit enters the room, a dark-skinned beauty, tall and refined with penetrating eyes.

"Fix her up something for me, please."

Tassit leaves the room without speaking.

Chapter Ninety-Seven

BRENDA IS VEXED. She sits up in the sofa bed. She is still thinking about how her dream of happiness had turned to horror in a matter of seconds.

"I don't want nothing to eat," she says.

Obese pushes away his food trolley.

"Ah, come on, you gotta eat something. You'll starve to death otherwise."

Brenda tries making her point. "I said I don't want nothing, yeah!"

Obese laughs, revealing rotten stubs for front teeth. He quickly changes the subject. "Say, how's your boyfriend doing? What's his name again? Yeah, Shun. I ain't seen him in a while."

"He's dead," Brenda bluntly replies.

Obese runs his chubby fingers through his long, greasy hair then belches.

"Do you know the only thing that is wrong with our lives is our death?" Obese lights up a weed and cocaine cocktail. He pulls hard and coughs even harder until phlegm comes up.

Obese motions his cocktail towards Brenda.

"You see this? This will kill yah." He laughs again, then smiles, "Yea," he continues. "Dying, once it takes yah it takes you for life. No more eating, smoking, or getting drunk. Yea, all those things that you love end up killing you in the end. Funny that."

"Yeah, that is funny," begins Brenda sarcastically. "Maybe that's why you like killing all those people you sell drugs to."

Obese's face turns dead serious and he puts his poison down in the ashtray.

"Now listen here, missy. I'm not no killer. I know everyone around here calls me, 'the fat blue-eyed devil.' Just because they and the government need somebody to blame for the problems which they made."

Obese scratches his testicles then leans forward. "Now listen. I don't use force or fraud to sell my product. I tell you straight up, this shit will kill yah. Unlike the government who get their bogus scientist to tell us a load of crap about our diets and watch us die slowly with carbohydrate poisoning. Look at me." Obese points towards himself then continues. "I'm dying here with everything underneath the sun. I got diabetes, heart and liver problems, my lungs are about to collapse, plus chronic obesity and no bloody teeth. And that's all from the sugary poisons which the government tricked us into buying. They made bloody addicts out of us."

Obese wipes saliva from the corners of his mouth, then adds, "But I came to realise that because we're all shit scared of dying we need an addiction to block out the one thing that's wrong with life – our death."

Brenda looks at Obese's stumps and feels sick. Tassit brings the food in.

"Nah, take it away, Tas, she don't want nuffing," orders Obese. He looks back over to Brenda.

"I got something to offer you, doh. It might kill you, but it's your choice. If you ain't got nowhere to go, you can stay here and I'll give you everything you want. On the condition that you give me sexual favours."

Obese scratches his testicles and continues. "When I want it and how I want it. You don't have to answer right now. Think about it for a few days." Obese struggles to lift himself out of the chair. His huge belly is exposed. He rubs it.

"Right, I'm gonna take a shit." He looks down at Brenda.

"Remember, that's the way the world works, nuffing for nuffing, that's the way it is." Obese leaves the room.

Chapter Ninety-Eight

BRENDA HOLDS HER waist and lies back in the chair. She closes her eyes and weeps silently. *Is this what it has come to? If this is what it takes, I'll do it. But that fat bastard is gonna spend some money.*

That's the promise Brenda makes to herself as the image of her crying child pops into her mind and her tears again start to flow. Brenda grips her waist and curls into a ball as she mumbles under her breath, "Mummy is coming for you, baby. Mummy's coming."

The days turn into months as Brenda stays on the sofa bed, giving 'the fat blue-eyed devil' her body and stacking the money he gives her. Then, late one summer night, it all changes.

Brenda stumbles upon Obese in the kitchen secretly unlocking his personal fridge. Right there in between the food are stacks upon stacks of money. Brenda's heart nearly pumps out of her chest as she realizes that the money she had saved together with the money in the fridge, her dreams of happiness will now surely come true. Moreso, it will be a good payback for all the disgusting things the fat bastard made her do to him.

Obese, unaware that spying eyes are upon him, locks the fridge and clumsily flicks the bunch of keys into his pocket and wobbles out of the kitchen.

Brenda quickly creeps back into the dining room. Tonight, no long ting; she's robbing the money and blowing.

Chapter Ninety-Nine

BRENDA HAD JUST finished pleasuring Obese. The time was 10.30 p.m. and everything seems to be going according to plan. She had scoped where the 'fat bastard' had placed his keys. Also, the 'bitch', Tassit was fast asleep as usual in front of the TV.

Brenda is ready. She steps out of the dining room smoothly, with nothing except the clothes on her back and her money stacked in a rucksack. She moves towards the sitting room and looks over at Tassit. The bitch is still sleeping.

Smooth and easy, Brenda steps into the opposite room were Obese lies, snoring heavily. She spots the keys in the ashtray on top of the windowsill. Quickly she glances over her shoulder and steps towards the keys.

At first Brenda tries removing the fridge key, but it makes too much noise in the stillness of the flat, so she grabs up the whole bunch. With the bunch held tight in her palm, she scopes over at Obese – he's still snoring. She steps into the sitting-room – the 'bitch' is also still sleeping.

Brenda takes two deep breaths and makes her way into the kitchen.

Chapter One Hundred

IN THE KITCHEN, Brenda has trouble with the fridge key. It's turning the lock right the way around without opening the fridge. Brenda swears, then hits the fridge. A voice from behind makes her freeze.

It's Tassit. She knew something was gonna go down because Brenda had left the dining room light on, and Tassit never went to sleep until that light was off.

Tassit goes mad – and it's horror. She throws the kettle. Brenda ducks and drops her rucksack. The kettle smashes against the fridge.

"You teefing, bitch!" Tassit jumps to Brenda with murder in her eyes. Her long nails grip Brenda around the neck.

"Oi, what's going on in here?!" shouts a half-dressed Obese. Tassit pays him no attention as she bangs Brenda's head against the fridge-door.

Brenda is screaming and kicking wildly, but the kicks have no effect on the strong muscular arms of Tassit.

"Okay, now, okay. Come on, Tassit, you'll kill her."

Obese peels Tassit away and Brenda slumps to the floor, barely breathing and holding her throat.

"Now tell me, what's she done, huh? Ay, Tas? What has she done?"

"The teefing bitch tried to steal your money, innit."

"No I didn't," protests Brenda.

"You lying little bitch. I'm gonna kill you."

Tassit grabs for Brenda. Obese blocks her with his wide frame. She shouts the words of a mad woman as her arms fly wildly up and down behind Obese.

Obese turns to Tassit. "Ah, come on, Tas, you know you have to chill out. Ah, come on now, let me handle dis now, yeah?" He turns back to Brenda.

"Now, Bee, did you try to take my money?"

"Nah, nah, I swear down, I didn't. I came in here to get a drink of water and the key was in the fridge. I was just trying to take the key out."

Obese looks towards the rucksack. He knows Brenda is lying, but acts as if he doesn't. He turns to Tassit. "You see, Tas? It was just a simple mistake." Tassit looks chilled. Obese thinks he has won her over and he turns back to Brenda.

"Okay, Bee, I believe yah. Just don't creep around the house again at night time, alright?"

Like a wild cat Tassit surprises Obese and springs onto Brenda.

"You lying little jezz! Come here, come here." Tassit pulls Brenda out of the kitchen by her hair. Obese wobbles after them.

"Oi, Tas, let her go."

"What!" Tassit's eyes are deadly. Obese goes dead

silent.

"Listen, yeah, she tried to teef your money, yeah, I want her out."

Tassit hits Brenda's head on the door then screams at Obese, "Open the door!" The door opens onto four-teen concrete stairs leading to the housing block land-ing. Brenda holds on for dear life, but her grip is slip-ping. Brenda tumbles down the stairs.

"Yeah, and go to hell, 'cause if I see you again, you die pon street." Tassit slams the door ferociously.

Chapter One Hundred and One

IN A DAZE, BRENDA stumbles down the rubber landing with one shoe on her foot and the other in her hand. She takes a rest by a short wall and puts on the other shoe. Her heart rate begins to slow down and she breathes easily. Tear drops bubble at the corners of her eyes, but the tears don't fall. Instead, a smile stretches across her face.

A new understanding of her world ignites in her brain with this thought: *God doesn't help people, people help people or people can choose to destroy people.* With this new insight, Brenda knows it makes no sense to go back home. Even if she did, it would be a waste of time. The government had repossessed the flat and boarded it up. Fasard had ended up in shelters and then on the streets, sleeping in shop doorways.

Brenda gets up from the wall and smoothes her hair out. She smiles again, remembering the words from one of her mother's boyfriends. *'A beautiful girl like you will never have to worry about money, as long as there are men alive.'*

Brenda brushes off her clothes. Her eyes are filled with stone cold determination.

She walks through the estate and heads towards the place where men congregate and stand outside their plush, flossed-out rides looking for loose women to prey upon.

Chapter One Hundred and Two

THE WINE BAR is jam-packed. Outside, plush cars line the road with people in them and surrounding them, all caught up in pointless conversations. As Brenda approaches the crowd, she gets cold feet and stops.

Before she can turn back, the plushest car she has ever seen shoots past her then slows down to a stop. It comes reversing back. She kicks out her leg in a sexy stance. The car stops with a jerk and the window rolls down. The street light reflects a face that looks familiar, but Brenda can't place it.

"Oi, one minute," the voice says. Brenda hesitates, but the voice persists.

"Oi, we're not gonna bite, you know. Just come here, man."

Brenda steps into the road towards the car. She can't see the driver's face, but his clothes are more mature than those of the passenger who is speaking to her.

"So what, are you gonna come in the bar with me and let me buy you some champs?"

Brenda blushes, "Ah, I don't know about that."

The voice questions, "Why?"

Brenda lies, "Because, I'm waiting for my boyfriend, innit."

"Yerrr, so how long has he been making you wait and risking such a beautiful thing like you among these wolves."

Brenda smiles. She knows the passenger thinks he's slick. She stays cool and plays him.

"Ah, not long, about half hour."

"What? He's taking the piss. You know what? I'm gonna be a gentleman. Come wait in the car."

The passenger opens the back door. The strong scent of leather hits Brenda in the face, and she pauses. The passenger continues his plea, "Come, babes, come."

Brenda jumps in and folds her arms. She looks over at the driver. He's talking on his phone and he doesn't turn his head, but the passenger turns in his seat towards her.

"So what you saying, babes? If your man don't turn up, what? We can have some fun, yeah?"

Brenda puts on her confused face and snaps her neck from side to side. "What do you mean by fun?"

The passenger shrugs his shoulders. "You know what it's about. Give mans some knowledge, innit."

Brenda falls silent considering her next move. She must make this person think that she's not a jezz, but would be his jezz if he's willing to give her what she wants. She applies her shocked face. "Nah, I don't know. I don't think I can do that. Anyway, I don't even know you. Brenda goes for the door but the passenger holds her shoulder.

"Oi, babes, just cool, man. It's not a hype ting, but I'm saying doh. You can't give man a bit of knowledge, a quick preview. Let me see what you working with.

Because you dun know I'm gonna roll up in the bar and buy couple bottle of champs' den we can bounce to my yard, bun some high grade and go for the second round."

Brenda smiles at the proposal. It is a start to pleasing him further, getting him hooked and taking whatever she can from him. Brenda looks at the expensive iced-out chain around the passenger's neck, smiles sexily then shrugs her shoulders with an implied "Okay."

The passenger slips around to the back seat– the driver is still talking on his phone, taking no notice.

Brenda gives the passenger head– he makes her swallow his semen. She wipes her mouth and licks her lips. The passenger zips up his jeans and smiles with contentment. He got what he wanted and now has to get away without giving Brenda nothing. He places his hand on Brenda's thigh, "Oi, you know what? Wait here. I'm gonna go to the bar and come back with ah couple champs and we're gonna roll straight up to my yard."

The passenger waits for an objection, but he doesn't get one, and without saying peace to the driver, he jumps out of the ride.

Chapter One Hundred and Three

THE DRIVER ENDS his call. For a moment, the inside of the car feels awkwardly quiet. Brenda is about to speak. The driver speaks first.

"Oi, come and get in the front." His voice carries the sound of authority, and Brenda jumps into the front seat.

The side of the driver's face comes into view. Brenda doesn't recognise it, but her dad would. The driver is Gize, the same Gize that had beef with him back in the day. Gize speaks without turning his head towards Brenda.

"He's not coming back."

Brenda looks confused, "Who's not coming back?"

"Him." Gize points at the passenger who is on his way over to his parked car. "And he definitely ain't coming back with no champagne."

Brenda looks out the window. Her heart turns ice cold and she stays quiet.

Gize continues talking, "Oi, do you believe in God?"

Brenda pauses for a moment before answering. She

shrugs her shoulders. "I don' know, I don't think so."

"I bet once when you was younger, you believed in him." Gize doesn't wait for Brenda's reply. "You believed that he would help you and give you the things that you want and when he didn't your belief began to fade."

Brenda's mind is in deep thought as Gize continues. "Then maybe there were times when good things happened that you didn't expect and felt that it must have been God. This then rebuilt your belief, only for it to be knocked down as everything good turned to horror."

Gize pauses and looks at Brenda out of the corner of his eye. "But check it," he begins, "think about the good things, who gave them to you? People, right?"

Brenda makes no reply, Gize continues. "Okay, think about the horror. Who caused it? People, innit? And who stopped it? Nobody, right? No angels, no God or Gods, nothing. So of course you're gonna disbelieve, because there is no evidence or proof for you, only for them who have family and friends that love and help them to succeed in life."

Gize turns himself fully towards Brenda. He grins before talking. "Listen, I wanna help you, I wanna help you get what their so called God could never get you. I'm gonna help you get happiness."

Brenda's eyes light up with intrigue. Before she can ask how, Gize tells her to 'shhhh' and just listen.

"There's a secret about this world. Once understood it gives you more power than any imaginary God. That secret is to provide happiness for others. Once you learn that, you control money and power, which can eventually bring you happiness. Of course, this secret has been used against you and billions of others for years by those who control the world. And as they get richer those who don't know the secret get poorer and die without ever knowing happiness."

Gize begins to laugh, then stops suddenly. He wipes the corners of his mouth then continues. "But you don't have to die without knowing happiness, because those who run the world need the happiness which you carry between your legs."

Gize rests his palm on Brenda's knee. He looks into her eyes and in a deep voice he says, "Let me help you to become their God."

Power surges through Brenda's bones and races up to her mind. She pictures her reunion with her child, both of them playing with a beautiful dollhouse, inside their new home.

As Gize asks Brenda a further question she snaps out of her trance, but the question doesn't register. Brenda merely nods without knowing what Gize asked. Gize takes the car off super fast from the curb.

Chapter One Hundred and Four

THE FOLLOWING DAY is warm and sunny and Brenda is feeling ready to do it. She walks down a set of concrete stairs in tight clothing, makeup on her face and her long hair scraped back and gelled down against her head, emphasising her features in full.

A soft red carpet leads to a large doorway. Brenda steps off the stairs and onto the carpet then slowly walks to the door. She stops outside and pulls down her expensive dress so that it hides her knickers.

The room is painted in white with priceless artwork hanging on the walls. A large conference table with tall leather chairs sits in the middle of the room. A connecting door behind the table opens and Gize walks in with a limp, supporting himself with a walking stick. He smiles as he pays Brenda a compliment. "Ah, you look heavy, come and sit down."

Brenda blushes and moves towards the table, "Um, Gary, is this whole building yours?"

"Yeah, all of it," begins Gize, a.k.a. Gary. "The whole tower block is mine."

Gize had bought the thirty-storey tower block from the government, who evacuated the tenants because of an accident that happened. The government wanted to knock it down afterwards and build new homes, but for some reason couldn't. Instead they sold it for the price of a five-bedroom house and now it's the headquarters of an empire providing sexual stimulation. There are over a hundred females working and living in the tower block. Eighty percent of the females are pretty pennies, because the hourly rate for each one falls between two hundred and a thousand bills. The rest of the females are rusty pennies – they used to be pretty pennies until they let the enjoyment of drugs smash and bend them into rusted ones.

The tower block is called Paradise Heights. The rusty pennies are housed in the basement. Above the basement is Wet Paradise, which has an oversized swimming pool and ten Jacuzzis surrounding it. Above Wet Paradise is a strip and lap dance club, and above the club are two hundred single rooms, called The Zones. On top of The Zones are offices, and above the offices are over fifty one-bed apartments that house the pretty pennies. And at the top of the block sits Gize's three-storey high penthouse. Gize had achieved all of these after serving five years in prison and placing two ads on the Internet. One offering females the promise of becoming rich, and the other offering men sexual stimulation from beautiful females. From those two ads grew an empire all controlled from the screen of his laptop.

Chapter One Hundred and Five

GIZE TURNS THE LAPTOP towards Brenda. "There's not much to this new century pimp game," he begins. "It's simple. All that happens is, the squeaks hit the website, choose which girl they want, pay by credit card, then come to the ghetto for their buzz of stimulation." The door behind the table opens and a woman with long legs and a tiny waist enters with a camera. "Yeah, plug it in over here," says Gize. The woman plugs the camera into the laptop. "Look here," says Gize to Brenda. "The pictures we took of you earlier are going to be uploaded now, live to the website, and within an hour, bids should start coming through. Because you're a new penny, the highest bidder gets to sample you first."

Has the woman uploads the pictures, Gize leads Brenda to the door with reassuring words. "Just relax and be yourself. Be cool. Remember, I've done all the hard work for you, all you need to do is stand at The Spot and stand sexy. Then when you receive a message on this phone, the message will either tell you the squeak is picking you up from The Spot or meeting you back at the tower. That's all you need to know for now. But remember to stay focused because those who don't end up rusted."

Gize flips open his phone and informs one of his top pennies, a girl named Ruse, who is medium-sized with mampy breasts, a slim waist and slender legs, that Brenda is ready to hit The Spot.

Chapter One Hundred and Six

THE SPOT IS sandwiched between a neglected park and forty rows of railway arches. The arches are either gambling houses or drug bases. Brenda and Ruse are one street away from The Spot.

Ruse answers Brenda. "Well, babes," she begins, "even though the squeaks know what you look like from the Internet, some are twisted bastards and they want it to seem authentic. You know, that little extra adventure." Ruse pinches Brenda's arm. "Don't worry, The Spot is safe for us pennies, it's just the squeaks that have a problem. Some rusted pennies have been clipping them. They wait until a squeak pulls up to The Spot and if the girl that the squeak has ordered isn't at The Spot yet, a rusty penny will rush the squeak and try a ting and sweet-talk him. If she gets through, she will give him head and then clip his wallet." Ruse adjusts her bra then continues, "I'm telling yah, babes, those rusted pennies are ruthless, they'll do anything. You've got to watch out for them."

They turn left and The Spot comes into view. Bright

neon lights decorate the outsides of some of the arches and women of the night line the pavement. Cars pull up and women jump in. Ruse leads Brenda towards her crew of girls, Cindy, Sweets, Juicy and Cerise. All are light complexioned with long hair; they look a bit like clones of each other.

Chapter One Hundred and Seven

"WHAT'S GOING ON LADIEEES?" says Ruse as she moves from girl to girl, planting kisses on their cheeks. When she's done, she introduces Brenda. "Everyone, this is Bee, the new penny on The Spot." Everyone looks at Brenda. Cindy is the first to speak, "Oh my God! She's beautiful, she's criss, innit you lot?" Everybody else agrees, they crowd around Brenda studying her like she's an extraterrestrial, asking if all the pretty long hair belongs to her. Ruse comes to the rescue, "Alright you lot, man, 'laow dat, man. Give the girl some space to breathe." The girls step off and Ruse pulls Brenda to her side.

From around the corner the infamous Queenie appears with Candy; two official rusted pennies. The atmosphere turns sour. Queenie and Candy walk past the girls with attitude. Queenie cuts her eye and sucks on her teeth. She and Candy stop a few yards away and begin talking between themselves. Ruse turns to Brenda and says, "Yeah, those are some of the rusty pennies. The only reason why Gary keeps them on is because once in a while a real twisted squeak would bid high for them. Other than that, they're lucky if they earn fifty bills for the week and because of that they're always hating on us pretty pennies."

Brenda's phone begins to beep. She opens the text message and the girls rush towards her. Cerise, the oldest of the girls shouts, "How much is the bid?"

Cindy shouts back, "I can't believe it, the bid's five thousand bills." The crew of girls burst into an excited uproar over the highest bid a new penny has ever got.

Queenie swiftly interrupts them in a drunk state and starts to shout. "You see, you see, it's not fair. How can dis new bitch just come on The Spot and get to earn five gees?"

"Innit, innit," replies Candy as she pulls down her shrunken jacket towards her hips and licks her fat, dry lips.

"And look at her," continues Queenie, squinting her beady eyes, "She's just a little girl and she's not even that hot." Queenie and Candy burst into laughter and clap their palms together.

"Oh shut up, Queenie," retorts Cindy. "Look at you, you're busted; that's why you can't make no papers. So just shut up and stop hating."

Queenie snaps her neck forward and bursts into argument. "Who the rass you talking to, ah?"

Cindy and her crew step forward as if to fight. "I'm talking to you, you broke down rusted skets, what?!" Cindy says as she pokes her finger at Queenie's face. Queenie backs off, "Ah, fire bun you anyway, that's why we been rushing and clipping you lots squeaks, yeah fire bun you."

As Cindy begins to reply, Ruse pulls Brenda away from the outbreak of a possible fight.

"Come on, Bee, you only have five minutes left to get back to the tower, forget about that." Ruse points towards the girls. "That's all long, you've got papers to make." Brenda leaves The Spot with Ruse and heads to the tower.

Chapter One Hundred and Eight

THE SHORT CUT ALLEYWAYS quickly bring Brenda to the tower. Any nervousness seems to have disappeared. Ruse has got Brenda mad focused and motivated with the understanding that whatever the bid, you get half. So two and a half grand for an hour's work drew Brenda right up close to her dream.

On entering the tower, Ruse walks up to the strip club. Brenda takes the lift to the sixth floor and steps into Zone Six, a reserved Zone for brand new pretty pennies.

Brenda sits on the edge of the bed and waits for the first squeak. Moments later, the door opens and a tall, dashing middle-aged man enters, suited and booted, wearing a white-collar shirt and tie.

He shuts the door and moves towards the bed. He stares at Brenda for a while then smiles, revealing perfect teeth.

"The moment I saw your picture I fell in love," begins the squeak, "that's why I outbid everyone, just to have you first."

Brenda feels that godlike power as goose bumps prickle her neck.

The squeak moves forward and continues talking. "You know, you're a very lucky girl. You shall get everything you desire."

He pulls Brenda towards him and for the next ten minutes has passionate sex with her.

When he's finished, he begins talking in a strange voice while he puts on his clothes.

Chapter One Hundred and Nine

"**FOR YEARS PEOPLE** like me have supplied people like you with your needs." The squeak does up the last button on his shirt and slides on his tie.

"We offer you hope and faith for that better life." The squeak pats down his tie on his chest, smiles and looks deeply into Brenda's eyes.

"And you love us for it, because you all hate life. Why do you hate life?"

Brenda doesn't reply.

The squeak continues. "It's simple. Because none of you are what you're meant to be."

The squeak puts on his jacket and sits in an armchair by the bed. Brenda has her knees up to her chin. She responds with a laugh, "So what are we meant to be?"

"The creator," the squeak continues. "But instead, you operate like a battery, producing energy for others, until you run down and die."

The squeak adjusts his cuff links. "You know, there is no difference between a road sweeper and an airline pilot; they both only produce work, and both are trapped as batteries in the system they produce for. This trap generates boredom, which leads to the need for any form of stimulation. That's where I step in and provide stimulation that takes away the burden of life." The squeak looks at his expensive watch, then continues.

"I am a very important man that productive people rely on for stimulation. I'm needed like the sugar in their tea." The squeak clears his throat. He stands up and sends a subtle warning. "I will not let anything get in my way to stop me providing this need. I hope I've made myself clear."

The squeak smiles then reaches into his coat pocket. "Shhhh," he says with one finger crossed over his lips.

"I know I'm not supposed to, but I can't help myself."

He hands Brenda a small bundle of money.

"Something a little extra. I'll see you soon."

The squeak turns on his expensive shoes and exits the room, leaving Brenda dwelling on his strange words.

Chapter One Hundred and Ten

BRENDA'S ATTENTION MOVES away from her present thoughts and towards the money. She stares at it, thinking what to do. She is about to hide it when the door opens.

Gize limps inside with blood on his collar. He has just come back from giving Queenie and Candy a beat down. Gize had tried for so long to get information on which of the rusty pennies were doing the clipping, but the rusty pennies kept a code of silence. They believed 'informer fi dead'.

Gize steps towards Brenda. His expression has turned from happy to serious. "The squeak gave you money?" he says.

"Yeah, I didn't know what to do with it," replies Brenda, in her baby girl voice.

Gize flips out his phone and tells someone to stop the squeak from leaving. He turns back to Brenda. "Alright, Bee, I know it's not your fault. Eya, give me the money. That squeak should have known better." Gize grips the money and stuffs it in his pocket.

"Squeaks like that are always trouble…"

Brenda cuts in, "He was talking real strange, I think he was trying to threaten me. And was saying su'um about the creator and stimulations. What does he mean by that?"

Gize grins then rubs his chin and answers, "Alright, Bee, let me break su'um down to you. In this world we have people who create stimulations and people who produce stimulations. So check it – your mum and dad created your sexy body through sex, and due to that you're able to produce sexual stimulation. But producing sex for a living doesn't go anywhere, because ten years from now you'll still only be a penny, and due to be a rusty one at that." Gize slides his hand softly through Brenda's hair and continues his fatherly speech. "Listen, you're gonna make a lot of money in this game, but you need to stack it and get out – don't get rusted. Focus and motivate yourself to a goal. Read books and learn, then someday you'll create a new stimulation that has never existed before. And on that day you will become a God."

Gize's phone rings. "Talk," he says. "Okay."

He looks at Brenda, who is in deep thought. "Get yourself washed, yeah, and get back down to The Spot." He points at her before he leaves. "And remember, don't take any money from no more squeaks, no matter what they say."

Chapter One Hundred and Eleven

GIZE CLOSES THE DOOR softly behind him and limps into the lift. In moments, he's in the basement in one of the backrooms. Four hunched bodies surround the squeak. He sits on a chair looking relaxed. "Please forgive me, sir," begins the squeak. "I was unaware of the time. If it's a matter of money I can pay."

Gize waves him down. "Nah, it's nuffing to do with the time. It's got to do with money. The girl told me you gave her some, is that right?"

The squeak's expression turns placid.

"You know that's against the rules, don't you?"

The squeak makes no reply. He adjusts his cuff links and remains cool.

Gize points. "But I know you don't care. You think you're overman because you offer false hope to those suckers who work a nine to five. I know about how you trap them in that illusion and let them believe you can supply their escape. But on the real, there is no escape. You know that and I know that."

The squeak grits his teeth. "What do you want from

me?"

Gize rubs his chin. "You should know that I know who you are. You're more than a very important man. The young girl that's upstairs doesn't know how important you really are and I can keep it that way of course, for a price."

The squeak swallows then flashes a devilish smile. "How do I know you won't talk even if I pay you?"

"You don't, but either way you're free paper bun. What do they say? You gotta have faith. Make a choice."

The squeak dips into his inside pocket. He pulls out another bundle of money. Gize waves him down. "No, you pay through the Internet. Oh yeah, add this to the payment too." Gize throws the other bundle of money to him.

"And make sure those two amounts go in every week plus the payments for any of my girls. You got that?"

The squeak's eyes flash with a hint of excitement, but he still remains cool as he turns on his expensive shoes and leaves.

Chapter One Hundred and Twelve

THE MONTH IS DECEMBER. It's been seven months since Brenda first stepped up on The Spot and bids have come in fast everyday, multiplying her money digitally into her private offshore bank account.

At this rate, Brenda feels she can retire within one year and by then she'll be old enough to legally take care of her child and live happily in that big house that plays over and again in her thoughts. This very thought plus listening to music and teaching herself to write songs gives her the energy everyday to bear the pain and not turn to hard drugs for relief. It even gives her the strength to fight the peer pressure from the other pretty pennies. Ruse, Cindy, Sweets, Juicy and Cerise, all sniff the white stuff and continuously offer it to her, but she refuses and sticks to catting out on her music and her new sense of life. This has built a super strong discipline, which she pieced together from the wise words of Sandra, the strange words of that squeak and the fatherly words of Gize. After hours of hard thinking all the words gelled and formed a whole, which made Brenda view the world and her place in it as follows: Provide stimulation for others and stack the money; use that money to educate yourself and develop your passion, create a value out of that passion and let a business trade that value for you, and with the money, create your own business. And once that business is grown, sell it and use the money to create further businesses.

For an almost fifteen-year-old, Brenda's ideas are profound. Since Gize's words have contributed most to her new way of thinking, she carries around inside her warm and happy feelings for him that spin into something close to love. She also sees Gize as her saviour, bringing her closer to her dream with every digital digit that adds to her account. And finally, the end will come where Brenda feels she'll be free from the harsh world of poverty and the forces that drove her to the grime of the hustle. What Brenda doesn't know is that Gize is planning a different end for her.

Chapter One Hundred and Thirteen

GIZE SITS IN a white room behind a large desk in a leather chair. He's tapping at a computer keyboard and looking up at the large monitor screen hooked onto the wall. Numbers come up on the screen. He gets a dial tone; someone answers.

"Yes, it's me," says Gize.

"Hello," says the voice.

"Listen, yeah. I've given you long enough. I want what we talked about."

"But we had an agreement."

"I don't care about that, if you don't want the girl to talk, you'll transfer the money now, within the hour."

"Okay, okay, calm down," begins the squeak with the expensive shoes, "I can transfer the money now. Open your account details and you should receive the money within ten minutes. I'll stay on the phone until this happens."

Gize opens his account and within ten minutes five hundred grand transfers into it. Gize looks amazed, but he doesn't speak.

The squeak clenches his fists together, smiles, and

wipes his sperm onto his chest then breaks the silence. "I hope this will keep her shut for good." He hangs up the phone. Gize leans back into his chair rubbing his chin and staring off into space. He then voice-commands his computer to summon one of his pennies. A short while later Ruse enters the room.

"Oi, Ruse, close the door," says Gize. Ruse shuts the door and walks over.

Without turning from the monitor, Gize speaks, "You remember a while back when I put the beat down on dem two chicks?"

"Oh yeah, Queenie and Candy. They will never come back on The Spot again, they're now catching dates near those red-bricked buildings."

Gize rubs his chin. "Yeah, yeah I know." He leans further back into his chair. "I want you to go down there and tell them Brenda informed on them."

Ruse looks puzzled. "Are you sure you wanna do that? Those girls will kill Brenda. They don't ramp."

Gize makes eye contact with Ruse. "Oi, bitch, do what you're told, 'cause you're lucky I don't make them know it's you that informed."

"Yeah, but, Brenda is your best girl, and she's part of my crew."

Gize nearly shoots out of his chair in a rage. "Oi, what did I just tell you? Mind I step in your chest. Go do what I tell you to do."

Ruse rolls her eyes, turns and walks away. Gize shouts after her. "Oi, make sure you make them find themselves to The Spot today, and call me when they're on their way."

Ruse makes no reply as the door hits her behind.

Chapter One Hundred and Fourteen

GIZE STAYS SEATED as he imagines his penis becoming hard at the thought of two prostitutes killing another. Although not very climatic, it will have to do because Gize can wait no longer for the squeak to snap from the blackmailing and murder Brenda himself.

From the first time Gize ran the blackmail on the squeak he thought it would be the last, but the squeak kept on paying. This made Gize mad, so he decided to tell the squeak a story that Brenda realized who he was and planned on going to the press if he didn't cough up five hundred grand by the evening. As the squeak transferred the whole five hundred grand, Gize's frustration rose at knowing that Fane's flesh and blood was still living and breathing while he could never again create his own flesh and blood due to those bullets that hit his legs. The first bullet grazed his groin area and left him impotent and seedless. The other bullet lodged in his leg and gave him a permanent limp.

Gize closes his eyes as he vividly remembers the time he drove past Brenda on the corner and his nephew mentioned that the drunk they had just seen pissing up his pants was that girl's father. Again, Gize wished that his penis could turn hard as he quickly reversed the car with thoughts of turning Brenda out, and when the opportunity comes and the time was right, having her killed.

Just before he stopped the car he had told his nephew to run the champagne bling on Brenda. It was the first time the nephew had tried the champagne con and was surprised that it had worked. After jumping out of the car he had rang his uncle Gize. Gize had ended the other call and answered it without Brenda knowing. His nephew then began giving him praise for the bling-con. Gize was telling him, *just cool, and was he sure about Brenda being Fane's daughter.* The nephew reassured him. Gize then got off his phone and called Brenda to the front. After he had dropped game on her, he asked if her father's name was Fane. Brenda had replied with a nod, so he was convinced as he drove away.

Gize snaps out of this sordid memory, rubs his chin, picks up the phone and sends a reminder to Brenda. It's time to hit The Spot.

Chapter One Hundred and Fifteen

IT'S ONE OF THOSE days that brings out a cold sun followed by rain. Brenda has been pacing up and down the concrete for the past hour. To her it feels like ten hours. She keeps looking at her phone asking herself. *Why won't it beep and where are all the squeaks?*

What Brenda doesn't know is that Gize had blocked all bids coming for her when he received the call from Ruse that Queenie and Candy were heading to The Spot. He texted all his other pennies to come back to the tower and then began accepting only tower block bids. So within ten minutes, Brenda was the only penny at The Spot.

Specks of rain begin to fall. Brenda retreats back underneath one of the railway bridges. A train rumbles and makes Brenda jump. She settles and calms herself and sticks her hands into her pocket.

A car cruises past her and she looks twice. She's sure it's the squeak with the expensive shoes. She looks at her phone but has no messages. It must be someone else, she tells herself. Brenda steps back under the bridge and adopts her sexy stance. Her thoughts turn again to her dream; running it over and again in her head until it seems to come alive right there in front of her. Brenda blinks her eyes closed, then opens them and jumping out of her fantasy.

She comes back to reality, thinking something is dead wrong.

Why no bids? And if that was the squeak with the expensive shoes, why would he come down to The Spot and just drive through? *Five more minutes*, Brenda tells herself, and she's heading back to the tower.

Chapter One Hundred and Sixteen

THE SQUEAK WITH THE expensive shoes approaches the end of Brenda's borough. He grips down on the steering wheel and spins the car around heading back towards her.

He has had enough of playing games. Although the blackmailing is the squeak's fetish, he knows if he indulges in it any more, the people who rely on him to provide them stimulation and whose money he takes to play his sick game will eventually discover the sickness and who he really is.

The squeak opens up the glove compartment to reveal his favourite weapon – an eight-inch hunting knife.

He accelerates as the rain bounces off the car. He turns on some music. The killing mode takes over, and as a hideous grin spreads across his face, he thinks of killing Gize as soon as he's done with Brenda.

The traffic lights up ahead make the squeak pause in his rhythm. Outside the window, he can just make out someone under attack. He doesn't know it yet, but it's

Brenda.

Cold stiff stares had been watching her from the park before the attack. She knew who they belonged to, but before she could say a word, there came pulls, punches and kicks by more than one pair of feet. They didn't stop the beating until she lay in a pool of blood, face-down in the pouring rain.

Chapter One Hundred and Seventeen

BY NOW THE SQUEAK has turned off his lights and pulled over to the side of the road as he waits for the attack to finish. He watches as Brenda stumbles to her feet and begins walking. He turns on his engine and pulls out towards her with the car lights shining brightly. Brenda stops and sways back and forth. She is about to fall when the squeak jumps out of his car. Brenda falls into his arms.

He puts her in the back seat and spins the car around, driving into the housing blocks behind the railway arches. He looks for the nearest abandoned home.

He lays Brenda down on the filthy floor in the broken down house, to end her life. The squeak kneels over her and begins talking in that strange voice.

"You have come to the end of your usage. You survived longer than the rest."

The squeak kisses Brenda's bloodied lips tenderly and continues. "You've done good and served me well. Your reward, of course, is freedom from this hell to an eternity of death."

Brenda quietly mouths, "Please God... bring me to heaven."

The squeak laughs through his nose. "Sorry, didn't I tell you? There is only one way to achieve real life after death and that's through new technologies that we don't have and we don't want. It's better this way. To remember nothing and to vanish into the darkness which is death."

Brenda wriggles and moans, then falls silent. For some reason she feels the squeak is right.

"Yeah, shhhh!" says the squeak. He pulls Brenda towards him and speaks in a low tone. "I know you only wanted change. I'm going to give you that because I'm good at giving people what they want. The horror of your life is over."

He raises his knife, but before he cuts Brenda's throat he whispers in a lower voice than before, "When evil disappears, goodness will reappear."

Then, with one stroke, he cuts Brenda's neck open. She lies there holding her throat, blood pouring out. Her eyes close and her whole life and what her future could have been flash before her.

The squeak smiles as he steps away, leaving another valuable, innocent life praying for something or someone to save it.

GLOSSARY

BER	Many
BITCH LICK	A ferocious hit
BLAZE	Gun shot
BLUD	Friend or Mate
BOOM-TING	Beautiful person
BOY-DEM	Police, Government, Ect
BREAK LEGS	Envious prevention
BREAKS IT DOWN	Success
BREEZE	(Depart) (Run)
BUN AND CHEESE	Chequebook and Card
CAT	Drug Addict
CLIPPING	Pick pocket
COLD	Good
COP	Buy
FLOSSING	looking good, ect
GEE	Gangster
HEAVY	Good
HIGH GRADE	The finest Cannabis
IRON BIRD	Helicopter
JEZZY	Jezebel or Slag
KETTLE	Wristwatch
LAOW	Allow
MAMPY	Big
MANS-DEM	Thugs
MURK	Murder, Kill
NEEK	Geek
PAPERS	Money
PEES	Money
PEEL	Rob
PEPPER	Gun shot
PICKNEY	Child
PLUGGING	Hiding objects inside the anus
PUSSYCLART	Swear or Curse word

RASS-CLART	Swear or Curse word
ROCK	Wear
SHINE	Oral Sex (Blow job)
SHOT	Sell
SHOTTER	Drug dealer
SKAGHEAD	Heroin addict
SKETS	Ugly or Slag
SPUNKED	Wasted
SQUEAK	Someone who pays for sex
STAR	Friend or Mate
STICK	Gun
STRAP	Gun
TER	An expression
TICK	Loan
WHITES	Cocaine
WIG	Head
WORK	Drugs
YA-NAH	You Know